The Size of the Dog

A novel based on the life

of

John Travers Cornwell VC

by

John Sutton

Prologue

June 1982

The pale blue Bentley Mulsanne drew to a smooth halt at the cemetery gates and a grey clad chauffeur leapt quickly out and opened the rear door nearest to the pavement. The elegant elderly lady who alighted smiled her thanks and, alone, made her way through the large open gates. She wore a light summer coat of pale lilac with a matching wide brimmed hat. She carried a simple bunch of a dozen pink roses and wore no jewellery but on the left breast of her coat was pinned a small enamel brooch in the form of a sailor dancing the hornpipe. After fifty yards she stopped before a large stone head stonein the form of a cross and anchor. She paused for a moment surveying the memorial, a smile playing about her lips as though she was recalling happy memories, then she laid the roses on the grave and slowly walked back to her car.

"Imperial War Museum, Ma'am?" The chauffeur asked.

"Yes please, Arthur."

Twenty minutes later the lady passed through the massive marble columns carrying another bunch of pink roses and crossed the foyer to where two large naval guns stood. A member of staff held aside a rope barrier that prevented members of the public getting too close to the exhibits and she went to the right hand gun and laid the posy on the left hand side of the large weapon. She then stood for a moment in quiet

2

contemplation. After thanking the staff member she walked slowly from the building.

Chapter One

June 1914

The boy was small for his age at four feet ten inches, small but stocky. Thick brown hair, like untidy thatch, topped a somewhat dour countenance that gave a misleading image of a friendly and humorous fourteen-year-old. A fourteen-year-old who was about to embark on a life of adventure and excitement, or so John Travers Cornwell thought.

All of his young life his one desire had been to join the Royal Navy. History lessons about Raleigh, Drake and Lord Nelson had fired this aspiration; although there had been a brief period when, after witnessing the guard changing at Buckingham Palace, he had considered the military. But the swashbuckling of the Elizabethans and the glory of Nelson's victory over the French had soon corrected that lapse.

England, in June 1914, was enjoying a glorious summer, and London in particular was basking in days of continual sunshine. The war clouds that enveloped Europe did nothing to suppress the high spirits that pervaded the great capital. In fact, a significant majority of the nation was looking forward to a clash with the Kaiser; to most it seemed inevitable and justifiable.

The previous day, Jack, as John Cornwell was known to his friends and family, had completed his full time education and was now returning home after achieving his lifetime ambition. He had enlisted in the ranks of the mightiest navy in the world, theRoyal Navy.With Bill Asher, his best friend, who had also signed on, he made his way home along Brompton Road through the Saturday morning crowds of shoppers and pleasure seekers.

The boys were opposites in many ways despite being firm friends. Bill was a head taller than Jack,

4

with flaming red hair and he worean almost permanent grin. His main problem was that he never stopped talking, and as his mother constantly reminded him, most of what he had to say was nonsense.Jack on the other hand was a boy of few words and serious demeanour, but the more observant would have seen a merry and mischievous twinkle in his grey blue eyes.

Their families were equally dissimilar. Whereas Bill had only one sibling, in his words, a snooty sister, Jackbelonged to a large family having three brothers and two sisters. The disparity did not end there, for Bill's father owned a chandler's shop just off Romford Road, and the family lived above it in a spacious flat. Jack lived in the poorer part of Manor Park in a cramped terraced house; it was the best that his father, a tram driver, could afford. By comparison the Asher's were well off but that did not infringe on the boys' lifelong friendship.

"This time next week we'll be in the Navy mate," Jack punched Bill playfully on the arm.

"Yep, and off to see the world," Bill grinned.

"Mind," Jack warned, "wiv the way things are, we could be off to war."

"So what," Bill replied with youthful bravado, "the Hun ain't gonna be no match for the Royal, now is he?"

"That's a fact, but hey, there's Amy," Jack said as they reached the junction of Walton Road, "Hi-ya, Amy," he waved.

Bill's sister returned his wave and crossed the street, smiling and looking more mature than her twelve years, dressed as she was, in the uniform of the Band of Hope. The plain cream dress and wide-brimmed hat set off her copper-coloured curls.

"What did you go and do that for?" Bill snarled.

"Hello Jack, I see that you're keeping bad company, "she smiled even more sweetly.

"Go an' boil your 'ead Amy," Bill glowered.

"We've been to enlist," Jack told herexcitedly, "in the Navy."

"When do you go?" She looked a little startled, even though it had been common knowledge at school; Jack talked about little else. You're so adventurous Jack."

"I've signed up too," Bill said, seeing an opportunity to benefit from some unintended approval from his sister.

Amelia acknowledged her brother for the first time, "You!" she laughed, "I can see father letting you. Anyway, you wouldn't have done it on your own, it's only because Jack has."

"I would too," Bill protested.

"Don't start you two," Jack mediated, "you always..."

"Hey look at that!" Bill pointed at a white, open-topped, Rolls Royce passing by in regal splendour.

There were few motorised vehicles in Brompton Road in 1914, apart from the odd delivery van. Most vehicles were horse-drawn, and so the appearance of such a magnificent motorcar turned most heads. In addition to the liveried driver, there were two passengers. The man, who appeared to be in his late teens or early twenties, was resplendent in army uniform, his Sam Browne and brass buttons gleaming in the bright sunlight, but for all his splendour he was outshone by his companion.

Until that moment, had Jack been questioned on the unspoken subject of the opposite sex, he would have listed Amy as a possible girlfriend in future years when boys gave up more interesting pursuits, but the vision sat beside the officer completely bowled him over. Her dark blonde hair shone like burnished gold and appeared to extend down to her waist. The breeze created by the motion of the car caused it to billow gently around her face. It was an oval face with delicate features and overwhelmed by huge blue eyes that met Jack's briefly as the car passed slowly by. She had been laughing at something her companion had said but when their eyes met the laughter stopped and was replaced with a slight mischievous smile.

Though their visual exchange was fleeting Jack felt that his soul had been touched and he stood open-mouthed as the car disappeared into the throng. Just before it was completely out of sight, hidden by the throng, the goddess turned in her seat and looked in his direction again their eyes meeting.

"Hmm," it was Amy who broke the spell, "she was pretty wasn't she, Jack?"Her words were brittle.

Bill saved the day, "Did you see her looking at me?" his face was flushed, "What a corker."

"Looking at you?"The brittleness had turned to a sneer, "she wasn't looking you," Amy scoffed.

"Course she was," he sought Jack's agreement which was swiftly given to cover his embarrassment.

"It looked like it."

Amy sniffed contemptuously, "Indeed, if she was, then it was out of pity or she is seriously cross-eyed."

"Aren't you gonna be late?" her brother snapped.

"You didn't answer my question Jack," her eyes bore into him.

"Why... what question was that?"

"Did you think that girl," she tossed her head in the direction the car had gone, "was pretty?"

"Can't say I noticed," he lied.

Her disbelief was written on her face, "Oh well!" she adjusted her hat."Yes, you're right for once, Bill, I am going to be late and lateness is a sin." She gave Jack a pitying look, "I will see you before you go, won't I Jack?"

"Yeah, course. I don't go till next week."

*

Jack sat at the kitchen table in a state of mild shock while his mother crashed pans on the hob and his youngest sister, Lil, sat across from him her eyes filled with pity and her heart with relief.

"Joining up indeed," Lily Cornwell said for the tenth time, "at your age, just left school yesterday." She continued to punctuate her words with pan lids. "Your dad's got you a good job lined up at Brooke Bond, an' you're taking it, like it or not." Another pan came noisily into contact with cast iron range, "you can help put food on the table, that's what you can do young man."

"But I get paid in the Navy," Jack pleaded.

Lily paused in her assault on the cooking utensils, "Yes, a measly seven bob a week to fight for King and Country and Brooke Bond is ten shillings and sixpence and that's just to start..."

"But, Mum, you know I always wanted to be a sailor, ever since I can remember..."

"Want and have are two different words my boy," she brushed a strand of hair that had escaped the tight bun at the back of her head from her flushed face. "We need your wage Jack, and there's a war coming, so that's two good reasons for you staying here," she turned and faced him, hands on hips. "End of argument, don't mention it again."

Short, rotund, and flushed from the heat of the cooking range, and anger, she faced her son daring him to continue the argument but his courage failed him. He slowly picked up the unsigned consent form from the table and went into the back yard. Lil followed him out and sat on the bench beside him taking his hand.

"Wait till Dad gets home an' ask him," she said encouragingly.

Jack gave her a feeble smile, "He won't go against Mum when she's in one of her moods."

"He might."

"Naw, he wouldn't dare."

There was a loud knock on the back gate and Bill entered with a crestfallen look on his normally cheerful face.

"My dad won't sign the consent form," he expelled a despairing sigh and joined them on the bench.

"Nor will my mum," Jack informed him with equal anguish.

A sullen silence fell on the trio;"Scouts tonight." Bill said eventually, "Are you going?"

"Don't really fancy it," Jack replied, "but I have to, it's boxing training, last session before the tournament next week."

"I start work in the shop on Monday," Bill mournfully changed the subject. He sighed deeply, "Imagine, working in a bloody shop when we should have been in the Navy."

"That's swearing Bill Asher," Lil admonished him.

"Sorry Lil."

"Well it's no better for me," Jack pointed out, "me dad's got me a job with Brooke Bond and I don't even know what it is. I could just be following the van horses picking up their shit."

"Jack!" Lil wore look of shock, and blushed at the word.

"Sorry Lil."

"You're both bad boys, if the boss of navy finds out you swear, he won't let you join."

The boys laughed and Jack put his arm round his little sister.

"Hello, hello!" Jack's father, Eli, came out of the kitchen with a mug of tea in his large hand, "Ere, push up," he settled himself on the bench beside them.

"Dad," Jack pleaded, "can you talk to mum, she...?"

9

Eli cut him short with a grimace, slurped a mouthful of tea, wiped his moustache with an exaggerated flourish, threw a furtive glance at the open kitchen window and then mouthed silently, "We'll talk about it later," and then in normal tones, "Well, Jack m'lad, its delivery boy for you on a shiny, new Thorneycroft van. What d'you say to that, ay?" His merry eyes radiated a warning as to the reply.

"S'pose it's all right," Jack replied heeding the caution.

"All right," Eli's leathery face took on a look of sham surprise, "all right, riding around in a smart automobile, out of the rain, out of the cold."

"It ain't really cold or raining right now Mister Cornwell," Bill ventured.

"Nor is it young William, but it ain't gonna be summer all year, now is it?"

The yard gate opened again halting further discussion on Jack's good fortune or the clemency of the weather, and Amy entered.

"Oh no," Bill glared at her, "what d'you want?"

"That's no way to talk to a lovely young lady," Eli admonished.

"Nor is it," Bill agreed, "but she ain't no lady, an' she definitely ain't lovely."

Eli tutted his disapproval, "You're just saying that 'cause she's your sister,' he turned to Jack, "I'm sure Jack thinks she's a lovely lady."

Jack began to blush and Amy cast her eyes down, "You're embarrassing me Mister Cornwell," she looked up smiling shyly, her eyes met Jack's and he hurriedly looked away his colour deepening.

"I'll have to get ready for scouts," Jack nudged Bill, "are you coming?"

"Mother sent me to get you for your tea, Bill," Amy said.

"Yeah, I'll call round about a quarter to seven," Bill replied to Jack's question.

"Tea's ready," Lily called from the kitchen.

"An,' about time," Eli stood up, he ruffled Jack's hair, "never mind Buller me lad, we ain't all dead yet."

"Why does your dad always say that?" Bill asked after Eli had left them.

"Well," Jack settled himself more comfortably glad to keep the subject away from Amy's comeliness, "it seems that when my dad was out in South Africa we were fighting the Zulus..."

"I thought we were fighting the Boers," Amy cut in knowledgably.

"Well it shows what you know, smarty," Bill sneered, "we were fighting the Zulus before the Boers."

"Yeah, well," Jack hurried on to prevent a prolonged row, "it was the Zulus, and one day a patrol of cavalry chased a group of natives into a patch of long grass. Half the patrol followed 'em and the rest went round to cut them off." He shook his head sadly to add weight to his tragic story, "The ones that went after the Zulus walked right into a trap and they were all killed by a big gang that was already hiding in there, and the others knew nothing about it till it was too late."

"Yeah, but where's this, "we ain't all dead yet' come from?" Bill asked impatiently.

"I'm coming to that," Jack retorted with equal impatience, "when the rest of the patrol got back to their camp they were all a bit down, losing a lot of their mates..."

"It was only to be expected," Amy sympathised.

Jack continued, "The officer in charge of the patrol was Major Buller, and he was later a general in the Boer War, anyway, some wag shouts out to him, what me dad's always saying; 'cheer up Buller mi'lad

11

we ain't all dead yet'. Well this makes everybody laugh, so from then on, when anyone hadthe dumps, that's what they said to each other."

Chapter Two

Nobby Clarke, a Welshman of angular appearance and dry wit, helped Jack accept the inevitability of his enforced employment and gave him some hope for the not too distant future. Jack was surprised how quickly his first week of employment passed. Nobby was an ex-soldier who had served with the South Wales Borderers during the Second Boer War and he was now a member of the Royal Fusiliers Territorial Battalion. Jack felt happy and comfortable in his company; he was funny and entertaining with stories about his days as a soldier.

"It'll be war before the years out, boyo, and then you and me both, will be off to serve the nation."He halted the big green Thorneycroft in front of the Greenwich branch of Dominion Stores.

"Me mum still won't let me join up," Jack sighed.

"Mams won't stop their boys going off to fight for King and Country once it all starts, and everybody else's sons are doing their bit," he turned off the engine, "but right now we have a big drop here and there's no time for moping and melancholy, out you get."

It took them more than an hour to make the delivery as the manager insisted on checking his order twice before he would sign for it.

"He's the same every bloody time," Nobby grumbled as he eased the lorry away from the kerb, "he's put us behind by a good fifteen minutes," he honked at a cyclist causing him to almost fall off his machine. "I'll have to have a word with my Megan to get her to have a word with Sir James."

"Sir James?"

"Sir James Carr-Langton, he owns Dominion Stores and my Megan works as a maid at Sikkim Hall, his London home."

"Blimey!" Jack said, impressed.

Nobby grinned, "We make a delivery there today, what d'you think of that?"

"Blimey!"

"I should have warned you not to bring any dinner," he winked, "Cook always see's us right on Friday's. Fair sets you up for the weekend."

Sikkim Hall was a large late eighteenth-century mansion set in extensive grounds on the south side of the Thames, opposite the Chelsea Embankment. The drive, which cut through large neat lawns, was lined with Rowan trees, their boughs heavy and bright with orange berries. Nobby halted the van at the rear of the house and handed the delivery sheets to Jack.

"Get that moved to the door, I'll be back in a minute," with that he was gone.

Although the order was a large one, for a private address, it did not take him long to move the six large boxes to the rear of the van, and then he waited. It was a warm day and in the back of the van it was even warmer. Jack went to the door and sat with legs dangling over the side, and dreamed. It was a dream of regret; he could have been sat with his legs hanging over the side of a great ship of war if his mother had not thwarted the dream. No, that was not true, if she had agreed he would be in some training depot possibly as far from a ship of war as he was right now.

"Hello!"

The voice startled him; the owner of the voice had approached without a sound and was now standing with the sun behind her so that her features were a little difficult to see, but he could smell her. She smelt of roses and lavender, and of scented soap and fresh summer mornings. He shielded his eyes with his hand, her face sprang into focus and his heart stopped. He was struck dumb. He was three feet away from the vision that he had witnessed in the passing Rolls and she was smiling at him.

"Hello!" he croaked and swallowed hard trying to generate some saliva.

"My name is Romin," she offered a slim white hand that felt like warm velvet, "it's Rosemary Millicent really but who could go through life being addressed in such a manner. I trust you have a more sensible one? Name that is"

Jack swallowed hard again, "Jack!" he still sounded like a bullfrog with tonsillitis, "Jack Cornwell."

"I knew that you would have a prudent name," she beamed, "when I saw you the other day, I thought then that you would have a sound English name, and I think apart from George there could not be a more English name than, Jack."

"It's really John Travers," Jack explained, amazed and delighted that she remembered seeing him.

"John is still very sound, but what is the origin of Travers, it's not a name that I am familiar with?" she seated herself beside him on the edge of the van.

"It was me dad's idea," he explained, "there used to be an Irish featherweight boxer called Terry Travers who was only little but a terrific fighter, and as I was only little he named me after 'im, hoping I'd be a tough fighter."

"And are you, Jack, a tough fighter?"she fixed him with a serious stare and puckered brow.

"I fink so, I'm in the boxing team for the scouts, and do alright, I win most of me fights, and I won the North London Juniors light flyweight semi-final on Wednesday."

She leaned towards him and the scent of her made him dizzy, "Congratulations. You look tough, John Travers."

"An' you look beautiful, Rosemary Millicent," he could not believe he had uttered the words and instantly began to flush.

She bobbed her head, "Thank you kindly, Sir. Promise not to call me by the preposterous name again and I promise not to call you Travers."

They shook hands again, "Done!" he said, "but Travers don't bother me 'cos he was a good fighter even though 'e was little, and as me dad sez, it ain't the size of the dog in the fight that matters it's the size of fight in the dog that counts."

"How wise and how true," she placed the thumb and forefinger between her lips and emitted a piercing whistle. Before Jack had recovered from the shock, of so prim and ladylike creature whistling like a docker, a small pi coloured dog appeared, panting, and leapt into Romin's arms.

"Well Jack Cornwell, meet Jack Russell, and he is a doughty little fighter, though I do my best to deter him."

Jack ruffled the dog's fur, "Hello Jack Russell."

Romin wrinkled her nose, "He isn't really called Jack Russell, that's his breed, his name is Puck, after Puck of Pook's Hill. That's a book by Rudyard Kipling. Do you read much Jack?"

"Quite a bit but I haven't read that, but I have read one of his, Kim, it was called"

"Yes I've read it. If you enjoyed that then you would equally enjoy Puck of Pook's Hill. I shall lend it to you…if you would like…"

"Keep a tight hold of that brute Miss Romin," Nobby appeared round the side of the van in the company of a pretty girl with tight auburn curls and wearing the attire that signified her occupation as a maid, "I don't want to be torn to pieces."

Puck wagged his tail furiously and yapped to be released.

"Kill boy!" Romin said, allowing her charge his freedom. The little dog dashed round Nobby's feet panting.

"I see you've met the lovely Rosemary Millicent." Nobby said to Jack.

"Nobby Clark, Puck won't need to kill, I will savage you myself if you use that name once more," Romin put on a sham scowl.

"Stop your teasing, Nobby," the girl slapped him lightly on the arm and then offered her hand to Jack, "You must be Jack, I'm Megan," from the lilt in her voice Megan was clearly Welsh.

"And my intended." Nobby kissed her on the cheek, an action that resulted in another slap, delivered with more force.

"Behave yourself, Nobby Clark; if Her Ladyship sees you behaving like that we'll both be in for it."

When Nobby and Jack had finished carrying the family's groceries into the kitchen and they had been checked by the cook, a lady with the demeanour of a drill sergeant and a heart of a doting mother, the two of them sat down to generous portions of steak and kidney pie with potatoes and vegetables.

Nobby winked at Jack, "Told you we'd be looked after 'ere, didn't I, boyo?"

Jack could only nod, his mouth being full of the delicious pie and his heart and mind preoccupied with his encounter with Romin.

"I shall find that book in time for next week Jack," she said before she left them to their food. "You will be coming again won't you?"

Jack looked at Nobby for confirmation.

Nobby grimaced, "Oh, I don't know about that."

"Stop aggravating them," Megan reproached him.

"You can be a beast at times Nobby Clark," Romin narrowed her eyes menacingly.

"I'll see what I can do; I can say no more than that." Nobby continued to infuriate.

"Take no notice of him, Jack," Romin said, "I'll see you next week."

"You'll be alright there Jackie boy," Nobby said as turned the van onto the main road, "daughter of a Knight of the Realm, she'll inherit all the wealth of the Dominion Stores and their tea plantations in India and Africa, well, with her brother and horrible sister."

"Get out!" Jack laughed, "a kid from the East End wiv a family like that?"

"Well, you never can tell, these modern times, anything is possible."

"Yeah, an' pigs might fly. Anyway who said I'd be interested?"

Nobby laughed, "Hey, a looker like her could be penniless, have halitosis and a wooden leg and I'd still marry her."

"I'll mention it to Megan next week," Jack grinned.

"Cheeky little bugger, I can see that I need to work you a bloody side harder."

*

For Jack, Fridays could not come round quickly enough and each time they arrived at Sikkim Hall Romin would appear and they would chat about things in general, their likes and dislikes and their plans and dreams in particular. On one occasion, when the van had a mechanical problem, she took him a walk round the grounds, pointing out her favourite plants and trees.

Though their meetings rarely extended beyond twenty minutes, they learned a lot about each other's preferences their respective families, and their hopes and desires. Jack discovered early on that Lady Carr – Langton would not have approved of her daughter's meetings with a working class boy had she been aware of them, consequently Romin ensured that her ignorance continued, and their friendship was also kept from her elder sister, Violet.

Romin's brother on the other hand had a completely different attitude on such matters of class. His opinions had developed since he had joined the army. His newly acquired point of view frequently brought him into minor conflict with his father and exchanges of greater significance with his mother and Violet. Clive's first real contact with the working classes had been when he had taken over his first command, a platoon of Irish Guardsman, a regiment that Rudyard Kipling would later describe as; *being racially and incurably mad.* Clive loved his thirty mad Irishmen and could in no way see himself as being their superior intellectually or morally, rather the contrary. Their spirit never failed them in the direst of circumstances and their selflessness had to be witnessed to be believed. All of this, he passed on to his young sister who shared his great quality of compassion.

Romin genuinely sympathised with Jack and his mother's refusal to allow him to achieve his lifelong ambition to join the Royal Navy.

"Clive, like most, thinks that war with the Germans is inevitable, so perhaps your mother will see things differently then," she said.

"Naw, she's already said that's a reason not let me go," he sighed, "Clive's lucky that your mum don't think the same."

"It's family tradition that the boys go into the army for a period. Daddy was in the Kings Dragoon Guards until his elder brother was sadly killed in a riding accident, and then he had to take over the responsibility for the family business."

"My dad was in the Medical Staff Corps for fifteen years but that ain't influenced me mum."

Romin laid a hand on his arm sending shivers through his body, "Cheer up Jack; I'm sure things will go your way eventually."

*

Tuesday the 4ᵗʰ of August 1914 was a day that not only affected Jack's immediate circumstances; it was a day that was to change the whole of Europe and a way of life forever.

They had just finished delivering at the Cooperative branch in Bermondsey and were heading back towards Tower Bridge when Nobby spotted an unusual amount of activity around a newsstand, at the junction of Abbey Street.

"There's something important "appening Jackie," he pulled the van into the kerb and stopped, "I won't be a minute," he jumped from the cab and joined the throng that bustled around the vendor.

Jack watched the people in the street conscious that something momentous was afoot. People were reading their papers as soon as they purchased them and were exchanging words with those around them. The tension reached him in his little cocoon, itwas almost tangible.

"It's war!" Nobby climbed back into the cab and tossed the newspaper onto Jack's lap, his face flushed with the thrill of the moment."That's us finished for the day Jackie, back to the depot."

"But we're only 'arf way through the round," Jack protested.

"Read that," Nobby nodded at the paper.

Jack did as he was bid; *The British Expeditionary Force is, at this very moment, preparing to leave for France. Although these seven divisions are the best in Europe and the military are confident of victory by Christmas, Lord Roberts is asking that all able-bodied men prepare themselves for the coming storm. All Territorial's are being instructed to report to their drill halls at the earliest opportunity.*

"So if it's over by Christmas I won't even be trained in time, even if I sign up today," Jack said mournfully.

Chapter Three

No amount of pleading could persuade his mother or father to change their minds. He suspected that his father was secretly sympathetic with his desire but was not prepared to face the storm that would break should he contradict his wife's ruling on the matter. Jack was desperate. It was not only that he was being thwarted in his desire but also there had been drastic changes at his work place. A week ago, on the fourth of August, Nobby had handed in his notice, and with thousands of others joined the Colours.

William Donaldson was Nobby's replacement driver and with his arrival the humour and comradeship that Jack had shared with the affable Welshman ended. Donaldson was a dour Scot who only conversed in order to give instructions and after the second day Jack gave up all further attempts to engage him in general conversation. But the final and crushing blow was the delivery to Sikkim Hall, any delays were resisted, it was just that, a delivery, it was over in ten minutes at most. Even cook's offer of food did nothing to mellow the recalcitrant Glaswegian and he refused the kindness with curt bluffness. As a consequence of this, Jack's innocent rendezvous with Romin ceased, and what made matters worse was that they sat in the van, no more than a hundred yards from the hall, to eat their lunch. But that very day events were about to take a turn for the better, and Jack's life was to change dramatically.

It was the fourth Friday after Nobby's departure, the twenty–ninth of September, and as usual the Brooke Bond van was parked in the shade of a large chestnut a hundred yards from Sikkim Hall. William Donaldson sat in the cab eating his lunch and reading the Daily Sketch, while Jack preferred to be in the fresh air, on the grass under the tree, watching the passers-by as they strolled along the wide grass verge that hugged the river.

Jack got to his feet, "I'm just gonna have a bit of walk," he told Donaldson.

Donaldson consulted his pocket watch, "Be back here in fifteen minutes or you're outta a job."

Men in uniform were now a common sight and there were a number of soldiers and sailors strolling with their wives or sweethearts along the riverbank. Jack felt a surge of envy and longing.

The large expanse of grass, that separated the tree-lined road from the river, was about a hundred yards wide and broken with patches of bushes of pink and lilac rhododendron, which hid areas of the bank from view.

It was the small dog, dashing from one of these clumps of foliage, that caught Jack's eye, and this movement drew his attention to the three people about a hundred yards beyond the spot where the dog had appeared. Although it was not possible to see their faces he could discern that two were clearly female. One, the slighter of the two, had long flowing hair and the other a crown of thick blonde curls. The third person was male, in army uniform, and walking with the aid of a stick.

The dog had reached the riverbank and its speed had not decreased, there was only one possible outcome and this was also apparent to the group for he heard a female shout a warning, and the girl with the long hair broke into a run. The soldier hobbled after her assisted by the blonde. Jack began to run as the dog disappeared from view over the riverbank and he heard her shout again. The girl was closer to the dog than he and just before she followed the dog down the precipitous slope he recognised her – it was Romin. The manner in which she went over the bank suggested that gravity had taken over and she was no longer in control of her descent. In a confusion of skirt, petticoats and flying hair she vanished.

Jack started removing his overall as he ran, just short of the bank he paused to pull off his boots. The soldier and blonde were closer now and in his peripheral vision he saw that the limping soldier was the man he had seen in the Rolls, her brother Clive. He was shouting something but Jack was not listening, he was concentrating on the important and dangerous task that faced him.

Separating the river from the shore was a ditch, with steep banks, about four feet wide and of six, or more, deep. Romin stood up to her chest in foul looking water, her hair plastered with mud and holding Puck out of danger above the water. The look of delight at seeing Jack quickly turned to one of alarm as Jack hurtled down the bank in his role as rescuer and entered the water with the same lack of restrain as the dog and the damsel he was intent on saving.

The force of his arrival resulted in both girl and dog being submerged once more in the filthy channel. All three came up spluttering and coughing and Puck, no longer having any confidence in either of his rescuers, swam for the bank but once there defeated in his escape by the vertical incline. Jack half swam and half waded the few feet to the anxious little dog and lifted him clear of the water and handed him to Romin.

"Jack?" Romin narrowed her eyes to see through mire that masked her would be rescuer.

He grinned, "No 'uvver," he offered his hand, "I'd 'ave been more use staying up there, wouldn't I?"

"What a mess we're both in," she laughed, "how are we going to get back up there?"

"Come on, I'll give you a push up," he took Puck from her, 'ere, gimme Puck," he looked at her for permission, "I'll have to chuck him up."

"Try not to hurt him," she looked concerned.

"Hello, are you alright?" Clive and the other girl were looking down at them; their worried expressions gradually replaced with ones of amusement, "Well, well, well, what have we here, water babies, or should I say mud-larks?"

"Very funny Clive," Romin grinned appreciating the comedy element of her predicament, "do something useful and take poor little Puck."

"Poor Puck," Clive protested, "he caused the whole problem in the first place."

The blonde reached down and took the filthy dog from Jack and then took Romin's hand while Jack pushed her from the rear, a task that embarrassed him.

With nobody in his rear to help, Clive had to assist in Jack's extraction from the ditch despite his injury, "Take hold of this," he reached down with his stick and with the assistance of Romin and the other woman, Jack was hauled clear of the ditch.

"Damn plucky act old chap, can't thank you enough," he pumped Jack's hand vigorously.

"It was nothing," Jack protested.

Clive and Romin insisted that Jack go back to Sikkim Hall with them to get dry and clean himself up. He could see Donaldson stood by the van looking in their direction and almost feel the man's displeasure.

"I've got to get back to work."

"Don't be silly Jack..." Romin began.

"You know each other?" Clive asked.

"Jack delivers our groceries," she explained.

"And that's my driver waiting over there, he ain't half gonna be annoyed."

"Leave him to me," Clive waved Donaldson across and spoke with him briefly out of earshot.

"Everything is sorted out," he hobbled back to them, "let's get you two home and cleaned up." He tapped his ankle with his stick, "War wound Jack."

The blonde girl snorted, "War wound indeed. He fell into a hole after leaving the mess, no doubt the worse for drink."

Clive put on a look of shock, "What a scurrilous and unjustified accusation to make about a soldier doing his duty," the girl snorted again, "This angel of mercy, by the way Jack, is my lovely fiancée, Tess."

She took Jack's hand and winked, "It's an accident-prone family Jack, as you've witnessed at first hand." Tess was barely five feet tall with a small upturned nose and blue eyes that twinkled wilfully.

Sat by the fire in the kitchen, being fussed over by Megan and Cook, Jack met, very briefly, Lady Carr – Langton and her eldest daughter, Violet. It was difficult for him to believe that these two cold and haughty women were even distantly related to Romin and Clive. And so alike were they that it was only their disparate ages that prevented them from being taken for sisters; even twins.

"I believe we owe you our thanks," Lady Carr – Langton's face did not reflect her proclaimed gratitude.

Jack got to his feet clutching the blanket, awkwardly mumbling words of dismissal and blushing at his near nudity in the presence of the two condescending females. Violet neither smiled nor spoke, but eyed him coldly.

"Jack delivers our groceries." Clive informed them breezily, trying to lighten the mood.

"Yes, I've seen someone like him in the grounds." Violet gave her sister a meaningful look.

"You've probably seen us chatting," Romin responded, accepting Violet's challenge.

Their exchange brought a withering look for Romin from her mother, "Well, Cook is taking care of things." She turned, and followed by Violet, headed for the door where she paused and turned back to face

Clive, Romin and Tess, "come along everybody, it is almost time for luncheon."

*

Jack made no mention of his exploits to his family that afternoon, but it was not a secret that could be kept for very long. The following Monday evening Alverstone Road was full of the news, news that a reporter from the Hammersmith Herald, had been to interview young Jack Cornwell at number twenty-seven. On Tuesday evening the story of Jack's heroics was the talk of Manor Park, and the added detail that he was to be awarded with the Boy Scout Badge for Courage increased the status of his sudden fame. The identity of the subject that he had rescued further enhanced his reputation to such a degree that a small column appeared in the Evening Standard.

"I wonder if you would have risked your life to rescue a boy," Amy asked peevishly.

"I'd 'ave done it for the dog," Jack defended himself a little angrily, "anyway," he added, "I didn't risk me life, the water only came up to my chest."

"Hmm!" Amy stopped and pointed to a news billboard, "they seem to think you are a hero."

"Well he was," Bill protected his friend from his sister's unjustified attack, "anything could've happened in water that deep. "Anyway," he continued pushing his face close to hers, "you're just jealous 'cos Jack saved a pretty girl."

Amy sniffed one of her contemptuous sniffs, tossed her head and flounced off to join a group of her friends on the other side of the road.

"Take no notice of her mate, she's just jealous."

"Jealous! Why?"Jack's feigned ignorance did not fool Bill.

"Garn, you know she's soft on yer," Bill pushed him, "always has been since infants."

"Get out!" Jack returned the shove, "Amy's more like me little sister," his flushed cheeks gave the lie to his protest.

When they arrived at the church hall, where the 11th East Ham Scout troop held their meetings, they were surprised to see most of the troop outside in the yard, and even more surprising was the Rolls parked by the kerb.

"What's going on, Slugger? "Jack asked his patrol leader.

Slugger grinned, his pugilistic features softening, "It's all for you Jackie boy. Lord something or the other is down 'ere to give you a medal."

"A medal?" Jack felt a rush of panic. The idea of standing in front of a lot of people and possibly having to respond filled him with dread. Before he could make a plausible excuse and flee, Dan Flaherty, the scoutmaster, was at the door and calling him over.

"Come on, Jack we're waiting for you," Dan did not issue requests, as an ex-company sergeant major in the Coldstream Guards; he was only comfortable giving orders.

Jacks discomfiture began immediately as the troop began to clap as he made his way reluctantly to the door, and the volume mounted when he entered the hall. Scores of people turned to face him and joined in the ovation. At the far end of the hall a row of chairs faced the audience and among those seated there he recognised Romin and Clive and sat beside them was another Guards officer. Beside Romin sat a dignified man with grey hair and a King George beard that could only be Sir James Carr-Langton, Romin's father.

The twenty or so yards up the hall seemed like a mile, he walked it in a complete daze. People were now on their feet applauding and the group at the end of the hall had done likewise. Jack felt that he was apart from his body – in another place, observing.

When everyone was seated Dan Flaherty stood to speak, though Jack, in his confused state took in virtually nothing of what was said. Then it was Romin's father talking and it was only the burst of applause that indicated to Jack that the speeches were over and his presence was required. Romin was now stood beside her father, smiling, her eyes encouraging him and in her hand was a small silver cross suspended on a piece of blue ribbon.

The hall fell silent and the sound of his boots was strangely loud on the wooden floor as he took the half dozen strides necessary to reach her. Suddenly he was returned to his body as the scent of her filled his nostrils. She adeptly pinned the Silver Cross Badge of Courage to his shirt as though it was a thing that she did on a daily basis; then she kissed him on the cheek.

"Thank you, Jack," she said, her words almost drowned by the cheer of the troop delighted by the sight of one of their number being kissed by the daughter of a knight of the realm. The next thing Jack knew he was surrounded by well-wishers and showered with congratulations and praise, he felt a complete fraud.

"It was nuffin," he kept saying but his words were either ignored or disputed.

"What you did took a great deal of courage, Jack, and that's why you're wearing that medal," Clive insisted. He beckoned the other officer across, "John, come and meet Jack. Jack this is John Kipling a fellow officer of mine."

Jack shook hands with the young officer who, even to Jack, appeared extremely young but he had taken steps to disguise his youth for an insubstantial moustache adorned his upper lip.

"I hope that I can find the courage to achieve that sort of recognition when the time comes," John said smiling shyly.

Later, as they were leaving the hall, Romin walked beside him a little way from the rest of them. "John is Rudyard Kipling's son," she said quietly throwing a look in his direction to make sure that he was out of earshot, "but he does not make much of it. His father's fame is a little too much for such a shy man."

"Gosh! Rudyard Kipling. If he was my dad I'd be telling everyone," Jack replied casting a look of admiration at the young subaltern.

"Well done mate," Bill stepped from the throng by the door and hugged him and then stood with an expectant look on his freckled face.

"This is my best mate, Bill Asher."

Bill took Romin's hand and bowed, "Pleased to meet you, Ma'am."

Romin squealed with amusement and curtsied, "Likewise, good Sir."

"What yer doing yer clown?" Jack scowled.

Bill looked hurt, "Well, she's a Lady ain't she?"

"Yeah," Jack agreed, "but she ain't the Queen."

Before any further pleasantries could be exchanged Amy pushed in front of her brother, hand extended, "And I'm Bill's sister, another of Jack's best friends," she threw Jack a look of defiance, "we've been friends all our lives," she added.

"Well you're very lucky to have such a nice and brave friend," Romin replied unperturbed by Amy's evident hostility. She turned to Jack, "I hope that I shall see you on Friday, Jack."

"Yeah, course."

"Father's calling, I shall have to go. It was so nice to meet you Bill," she smiled sweetly at Amy, "and you also, Miss Asher."

Jack and Bill watched her get in the Rolls with her father and the two Guards officers with unconcealed awe; Amy sniffed.

29

Chapter Four

The war was not over by Christmas as had been predicted, nor was there any sign of an end. The start had been less than conspicuous. Belgium had collapsed, a French Commandant, Wolff, had been executed having surrendered his command only two weeks into the war, and the British Expeditionary Force had retreated at Marne. Now the opposing forces faced each other in static positions, trenches that extended from the Belgium coast, at the estuary of the River Yser, to the border with Switzerland, creating trench works over four hundred miles long. This state of affairs would exist, more or less without change, for the next four years.

The months passed quickly, there is little dullness living in a nation that is occupied in total war. Everyone read news bulletins avidly from the navvy repairing the road to the lord in his stately home; for everybody in the land had a relative or friend involved in the bedlam being acted out across the English Channel.

For those at home the telegraph boy, in his blue uniform and riding his red bicycle, had become as feared as the Hun's artillery was by those in the trenches, for the fresh faced youths invariably brought the dreaded news of a loved one lost. Every school and factory in the land displayed lists of former pupils and work mates who had fallen. Some towns and work places lost half of their young men in single battles because of the ill-fated Pals Battalions. These individual battalions of regiments were formed where the pals from one town, or large work force, provided sufficient volunteers to create a single battalion of a thousand men. Towards the end of the war even those considered too small to join the army in 1914, were permitted to raise their own battalions and were known as the Bantam Battalions. They fought with great distinction despite the diminutive stature of those who filled their ranks.

To Jack, the weeks and months flew by for he lived with the constant fear, despite the facts, that it would all end before he could enlist and join the fray. So many things were changing all around him. Dan Flaherty, the scoutmaster, had re-enlisted and left the troop along with a number of the older boys, but worst of all, his elder brother, Arthur had enlisted in the Middlesex Regiment. At first Jack had seen this as being to his advantage as it would weaken his mother's stand. Unfortunately Lily did not see it in quite the same way and steadfastly refused to change her position.

However, in late June, Jacks fortune was to change. The moment that he arrived home from work he knew that something was amiss. Despite it being a warm evening there was a distinctly frosty air in the kitchen of 27 Alverstone Road. His father was sitting at the kitchen table reading the evening paper and normally he would not have been home at this time when he was on the late shift.

Another clue to possible discord was his sister Lil, she had taken up a position opposite Eli and was staring at him with a worried expression, the expression she wore when she felt the need to act as peacemaker.

"You're 'ome early, Dad?" He ventured, spotting too late the grimace of warning from Lil. Eli looked up from the paper but before he could reply Lily turned from the kitchen sink, her face like thunder.

"Home early," she almost screamed, Lil winced, "home early," she stabbed the large kitchen knife that she had been washing in the direction of her husband, "this ain't his home anymore is it Eli Cornwell?"

"Don't be daft woman," he turned the page of the paper noisily.

"Don't be daft!" her voice went up a couple of decibels, "who's the daft one Lil, go on tell me that?"

Lil cringed, "Mum," she pleaded

"You tell 'im then," she addressed her husband again, "go on, you tell him who the daft one is," Eli made to speak but she continued, "D'you know what this daft old sod's gone and done?"

"Mum, don't swear," Lil pleaded.

"Swear, swear, he's enough to make a bleeding Saint swear," she stood with one hand on her ample hip and the other clutching the vicious looking knife, "he's only gone and joined up again, I ask yer, sixty bloody years old and he goes an' joins up again. And the army takes him, a decrepit old man."

"'Ere," Eli got to his feet angrily, "don't you call me decrepit, woman, I'm as fit as many fellah's half my age."

"Yeah, an' fellah's half your age are still old."

"I've had enough of this; I'm off to the pub," he grabbed his cap from the hook on the door and went out slamming the door behind him.

"Yeah, that's right, desert your family," she screamed at the door. The light of hope must have been bright in Jack's eyes for her next attack was directed at him. "And you needn't get any ideas about going, your wage is more important than ever now."

Jack caught up with his father just as he was about to enter the Bear and Dog, "Dad," he called, breathless from the run.

"Oh Gawd, I know what you're after," Eli sat down wearily on the bench by the door to the pub and Jack sat beside him.

"Dad, you've got to let me join now."

"Jackie, it'd kill yer mum if you go too," he placed a comforting hand on his sons shoulder, "your time will come."

"It'll all be over before I'm twenty-one," he shrugged off his father's hand peevishly.

"I should bloody 'ope so."

"Well then!" He got to his feet, angry now. "It ain't fair, Arthurs doing 'is bit and now you're going too. It just ain't fair."

"Sit down," Eli took his sons hand and pulled him back to the bench, his face serious and displaying the pity that he felt for his son, "You really wanna go don't you, Jack?"

"Well course I do Dad, even wivout this war, you know I've always wanted to be a sailor," Jack sensed the first rays of hope.

"Was a time when I hoped you'd be a soldier like your ol' man," Eli gave a wry smile.

Jack spotted the opening, "I'll join the army if you want me to."

Eli laughed and ruffled Jack's hair, "Cunning little sod. Go on, I'll sign your papers."

Jack leapt to his feet unable to suppress an almost girlish squeal of delight, and threw his arms around his father's neck, "Oh, thanks Dad, you don't know how much it means to me."

Eli smile, "I think I do, Jack, even your mum does," he raised a finger of warning, "Mind, not a word to her about this…, well not until it's all done and dusted."

"Scout's, Honour," Jack raised three fingers in the scout salute. Suddenly the aura of joy slipped from him and he became solemn, "I'll make you proud of me Dad," he put his arms round his father again.

"I already am proud of you son," Eli patted Jack's back unable to keep the catch from his voice.

*

As far as her family were concerned, Sarah had married beneath her when she had married Thomas Asher a hardworking and God-fearing Dorset man. They had met through their service with the Salvation Army and both were still very active in this cause despite running their successful little business and raising their two

33

children. Sarah's strong faith showed in her face and in her many acts of kindness, but despite these saintly qualities she was a strong willed woman who was not to be crossed. She ruled her home with all the discipline of a guards drill sergeant but tempered with the compassion and love of a mother.

Amelia had been blessed with her mother's looks and much of her temperament, but in her, the toughness outweighed the benevolence. If it had not been for the red hair it would have been reasonable to have assumed that Bill was an adopted child for he displayed few of his parent's qualities. The most noticeable difference was the volume of noise that he could create with such little effort. In a calm, quietly spoken family Bill was something of a fly in the ointment. His parents were tolerant but strict and Amelia was constantly at war with her elder brother. His effect on others went unnoticed by Bill, even when his irritating behaviour was pointed out, and Amy did this constantly, it made little impression on him, if anything he found it amusing.

He went into the shop as his father was preparing an order of nails and screws for a local joiner, "Wanna a hand with that Dad?" he asked hoisting himself onto the counter.

His father looked up and smiled, "Well you're not much use up there are you?"

"What d'you want me to do?" he dropped to the floor.

Thomas winked at his customer, "Forgive my doubting your good intentions, son," he pushed a box of nails along the counter."Weigh a pound of those," he added, "but your sudden urge to volunteer for work makes me suspect that, either you have committed some act of which I may not approve and it is about to come to my attention, or there is something that you want." He winked again at the shopper who grinned and they both waited with interest for Bills reply.

Bill cleared his throat and kept his back towards his father as he poured the nails onto the scales, "A pound, did you say dad?"

"A pound," his father confirmed.

Bill carefully poured the nails into the brass dish on the scales conscious that his father and the man were watching him.

"Mister Cornwell popped in earlier," Thomas said.

Bill turned to face his father and in doing so spilled nails onto the counter, "Oh!"

"He told me that he has given his permission for Jack to join the Navy."

Bill gulped, "Oh!" was all he could manage, and his nerve wavered.

"So!" His father began totting up the man's bill, his pencil tracing down the list as he added the amounts in his head. He wrote the final amount and passed the paper to the man, "did you know that Jack now had his parents' consent?"

"Hmm, well... yes," Bill felt the sweat beginning to run down his back.

"Two and four pence please," Thomas said to the customer.

The customer, grinning, handed over a half crown and Mr Asher gave him two pence change, never taking his eyes of Bill.

"Well?"

"Well," Bill swallowed hard and slowly drew a folded piece of paper from his pocket. Sheepishly, he pushed it across the counter towards his father averting his eyes, "I, er..."

His father took the form just as his mother entered the shop from the living area bearing a mug of tea for her husband.

"Good morning Mister Painter," she greeted the customer who was clutching his purchases and still engrossed in the unfolding drama.

"Oh! Morning Missus Asher," he touched the peak of his battered cap.

"What have we here?" Sarah peered over her husband's shoulder at the sheet of paper that he was reading. She turned her green eyes onto her unusually silent son, "Are you wanting to leave us Bill?" she asked softly.

Bill stared at worn pine planked floor wishing desperately that it would open and engulf him and his loss of nerve.

"Well, not really," he muttered.

"This would seem to indicate that you do," she took the form from her husband and crossed the shop to her son and put her arms round him, and hugged him, "We'll give our consent Bill," she stood back holding him at arm's length and smiled at his shocked expression, "It wouldn't be fair to let Jack go alone and break up a lifetime friendship." Tears filled her eyes as she shook her son gently, "Don't look so gormless Bill," she turned to Mister Painter, "our son is about to join the Navy," she explained.

Mister Painter grabbed Bills hand and shook it furiously, "Well done boy, well done," he turned to Thomas, "You must be really proud o' this young chap, Mister Asher."

"We are," Thomas clasped his son to his chest and, with misting vision, added, "proud, but just a little sad."

With a sinking heart Sarah watched a telegram boy lean his bicycle against a lamppost across the road and knock on the door of Rose Miller whose young husband was away with the army in France, she knew the news would not be good.

*

"I am pleased for you Jack," Romin took his hands in hers, "but I can't say that it makes me happy"

It was late evening and still very warm even though the sun had dipped behind the garden wall and they sat in shadow. They were sitting in the pergola by the rose garden, hidden from the house. Jack had borrowed a shilling from his eldest sister, Maud, to make the journey across London and give Romin the news of his enlistment and say goodbye.

"It makes me a bit sad," Jack admitted, "leaving me family an' all," he squeezed her hands and added shyly, "and leaving you."

"That's sweet, thank you," she smiled sadly;"I shall certainly miss your visits brief though they've become."

For a while they sat in silence holding hands and each with their private thoughts, fearful and hopeful.

"Nobby has been promoted to Corporal," Romin broke the silence, "and is hoping to get a spot of leave."

"Oh! That's good, when is he due home?"

"Megan only got the letter yesterday and he wasn't specific about a date," she sighed deeply. "Clive's company has moved back up into the front line again."

"Well it ain't been much fun where they were, "as it, lots of fatigues and stuff."

"No, not really, and although they have supposedly been out of the line the regiment have still suffered twenty-two wounded and one death from the shelling," she paused for a moment, "and now I've got two of you to worry about."

At nine, when the warm evening was beginning to cool, he took his leave after promising to write regularly.

"I discussed that eventuality with Megan and she has suggested that you send your letters via her to avoid any difficulties with mother."

*

Platform two at Paddington station was particularly busy with servicemen on the morning of the 27th of July

1915, most of them sailors returning to Plymouth after a period of leave or a course. They were joined by scores of new recruits setting forth on their new lives, some calmly, some eagerly but all with a dash of trepidation. Jack and Bill did their best to hide their impatience as their respective mothers fussed about aired laundry and eating healthily. Fathers gave last minute advice about how to keep on the right side of officers and NCOs and the dangers of strong drink. Jack had the added irritation of little Lil's grief at his parting, she clung to his middle with her head pushed against his chest, her slight body wracked with sobs.

"It's gonna be alright, Lil, I'll be home for leave at Christmas," he patted her head but her lamentation went unappeased.

Conversation was difficult and stilted, sadness hung over them like a cloud. The two boys stood by the open door of the carriage, clutching their small packages of personal belongings, and were constantly forced to make way for other passengers. The small talk petered out and the engine immersed itself in a cloud of noisy steam.

"We better get on," Bill said.

They leaned out of the window, Jack stretching down to hold Lil's hand until the very last moment. Each door was surrounded by families, most in tears, as they bade farewell to their loved ones, who in turn endeavoured to offer words of solace. From his elevated position Jack spotted a familiar form, flawless in his grey uniform, it was the Carr – Langton's chauffeur, Sir James must be catching a train. Then he saw the two females, Megan and Romin. He waved frantically and called her name but the noise of the crowd and fiery engine drowned his words. It was Megan who spotted him and the chauffeur forced away through the throng. Megan and Romin stopped and spoke to Amy, her being the only person that Romin recognised, but the noise drowned their exchange. Then, followed by Amy, they eased their way closer.

"I hope you will forgive our coming, Jack," Romin shouted above the racket, "I'll be brief; I don't want to intrude on your family's good-byes."She eased forward a little more and reached up and touched his arm, "I would like to meet your mother. Is she here?"

"Amy," Jack called, "will you introduce Romin to my mum?"

Amy pulled herself up on the step and kissed him on the cheek, "Of course," she turned back to Romin with an expression of victorious smugness, "I'll introduce you after, when the train has left."

Romin smiled graciously, "Thank you."

The remaining doors crashed shut; the engines shrouded itself once more in a cloud of steam, the porters whistle shrilled and the train lurched into motion.

The boys remained waving out of the window until a slight bend in the track hid the families from view.

Chapter Five

HMS *Vivid* was housed in Keyham Barracks, on a rise that overlooked Plymouth Sound. The Royal Navy had taken possession of it in 1889 after much wrangling. It was an imposing collection of buildings, constructed in limestone and dressed in Portland stone. It could house 6000 men in three majestic accommodation blocks. There was also an administration block, an officers' wardroom, squash courts, a gymnasium and a swimming pool. Facing the main gate was an impressive clock tower and flanking it was, on the right, the Commodore's house and on the left the guardroom, both of these building had a sobering effect on those who passed through the gate, whether sober or inebriated.

Thirty-four youths had marched the two and quarter miles from the railway station under the critical eye of one William Eaton, Corporal of Royal Marine Light Infantry. William Eaton was nearing the end of his service, he was in his twenty-first year with the Corps but the two medal ribbons on his broad chest did not give a fair impression of his service. Until he had received the red and yellow ribbon for his brief tour in Gallipoli the previous year, the green and white representing the Boxer Rebellion had been his only medal. Despite this lack of silverware Bill had served on four continents visited six and sailed the seven seas.

His current posting as a drill instructor had been greatly against his wishes but the wound that he had received at Gallipoli had meant that he had been medically downgraded and was unfit for active service, a devastating blow to long term soldier. A large piece of shrapnel in the left shoulder had restricted the use of his left arm but he was perfectly able to carry the silver topped cane, the badge of a drill instructor, tucked under his partially crippled arm and those who did not know of his wound retained their ignorance. The wound had not affected his overall fitness as the newly arrived recruits could attest, for they had covered the two and a half miles in a little over thirty five minutes and at this speed William Eaton had considered them 'idle'. It was also apparent that his voice had not been affected by his injury.

"Put yer kit down, remain in three ranks and keep yer gobs shut," he snarled. They had halted on the huge drill square in front of the administration block and apart from squads of men being drilled at the far side of the huge square, there were also two other groups of nervous looking civilians already formed up when they had arrived. Corporal Smith went off to confer with their custodians.

"This is some bloody place," the boy who had marched between Bill and Jack observed looking around in awe.

"It is a bit special ain't it," Jack agreed

"Where you from, mate?" Bill leaned forward to peer round Jack.

"Newcastle. Why?"

"Just that yer twangs, bit odd," Bill explained.

"Aye, well, you'd sound a bit odd up on Tyneside," the boy said defensively.

"Take no notice of 'im mate, every time he opens his mouth 'e puts his foot in it." Jack offered his hand, "My names Jack, an' Mister Tact 'ere, is called Bill."

"Nice ta meet yer lads, I'm Ronnie, Ronnie Raven..."

Ronnie's sentence was cut short by an incomprehensible scream that was a mixture of rage and hopeless despair. The three of them turned in the direction of the exclamation of revulsion, and observed, for the first time, the majestic form of Chief Petty Officer, Dara Fitzgerald descending the steps of the

41

admin block, his pace stick held before him like the sword of Damocles.

"Corporal Eaton!" he screamed.

"Sah!" the NCO crashed to attention.

"Dose 'orrible little creatures was talking on my parade ground, so they were, get their bloody names."

As if by magic the marine Corporal appeared in front of the petrified boys and it was Jack who bore the brunt of his wrath.

"Who told you, you could talk?" he pushed his face within inches of Jack's, "you insubordinate bloody dwarf." Unlike the CPO he did not scream, he growled menacingly. "I will tell you this you short-arsed little nozzer, I will be keeping my eye on you and I promise you that I'll give you more to bloody-well fear than the Kaiser an' all his hordes of "airy arsed Huns," his voice rose from a growl to a bellow, "Do I make myself clear?"

"Yes Sir," Jack could barely form the words.

The raging corporal was not appeased; he tapped his stripes with his cane, "What are these?"

"Stripes, Sir."

"An' what does stripes mean?" he sneered.

"Uhh..."

"Tell 'im," he thrust his cane under Bills nose.

Bill gave the same answer, "Uhh.."

"It means I'm a corporal you bleeding gobshite."

"Have yers got their names, Corporal Smith?" the CPO halted in front of the squad.

"Just doing it, Sir," he drew a notebook and pencil from the breast pocket of his tunic.

CPO Fitzpatrick was a tall man, six feet and three inches, slim and as straight as the pace-stick that he always carried. Since being posted as chief instructor at *Vivid*, he had cultivated a sneer that made even the most confident recruit feel that he was not fit to set foot in this illustrious setting. Fitz, as the CPO was known, had a set speech that he delivered to every intake so as to establish in their minds the lowliness of their position.

He began to pace along the front rank eyeing his new charges with undisguised disdain, "Where in God's name did yous foind this bunch o' tramps and vagabonds, Corporal Eaton? What have Oi told yous about press ganging the inmates of asylums and workhouses, will you look at 'em. Oi've never seen such a bunch of scruffy and smelly individuals in all my... What in God's name is dat?" he pointed his stick at Ronnie's bundle of possessions that lay at his feet.

"Me things, Sir," Ronnie said with a trace of defiance.

"Your t'ings," Fitz echoed with exaggerated incredulity, "your t'ings," he poked Ronnie's meagre bundle of possessions with his stick."Blackbeard da pirate would not have allowed 'dis loathsome mess onto his disgusting vessel for fear of the plague, an' you have de audacity to bring it onto one of His Majesty's ships. What's yer name boy?"

"Raven, Sir."Ronnie was visibly shaking.

"Well, Raven me lad, I'm t'inking that you'll be getting your wings clipped in the next few months, so you will."He took up position in front of the three groups and raised his voice so that could all hear him "My name is Chief Petty Officer Fitzgerald and it is my unenviable task to turn yous horrible unwashed civilians into sailors dat are fit to serve in His Majesty's Navy, the finest navy in the world." He turned to his three RMLI corporals who had gathered behind him, "I t'ink gentlemen that we've met our match this time."

Jack had recovered from the verbal assault and his attention was attracted to a small group of sailors stood at the edge of the square, behind the NCOs. One of them, a tough looking youth, was miming to the CPO's words much to his companions humour.

"If we can transform dis rabble into baby sailors, then we'll have all earned knighthoods, so we will," he nodded to the NCOs, "Carry on." And then without another word he marched smartly back to the admin block.

Their place in the hierarchy had been established, their ego's had been shattered, now began the task of building them up into characters that could withstand the demands and adversity of naval life and war.

The youth that Jack had seen mimicking the CPO was Boy First Class James Cook, Jimmy to his friends. Jimmy had completed his training earlier that year but had been held back at *Vivid* to assist with the next intakes training. He had been allocated Hardy Mess, the mess in which Jack and Bill had been placed.

It was Jimmy's task to help them with the day to day business of navy life; how to sling and lash hammocks, how to stow their kit, iron uniforms, launder their clothes and all of the other tasks that are required of a young sailor that are not dealt with on the training programme. Jimmy was their mother hen; it was not a job that he relished.

"I was down ta join HMS *Birkenhead*, a new light cruiser," he explained as he demonstrated how to sling a hammock, "but her commissioning date has been put back, so I'm stuck wi' you lot, a nursemaid," he finished slinging the hammock, "That's how it's done; I'll leave it up so you can look at it tonight when you're slinging your own," he winked and grinned. "I bet some of yers wake up tomorrow wi' your arses touching the floor." He placed his cap on his mass of untidy black curls, "Right get fell in outside, yer getting all yer kit issued at 1500."

Their new home was a large airy room that housed sixty ratings in two rows of hammocks that were neatly lashed and stowed during working hours. One wall comprised of large windowsalong whichwere lined a number of scrubbed table and benches; this is where the boys would mess.

Despite their harrowing welcome they soon settled into their new life and Jimmy was largely instrumental in their transformation from civilian to naval life. As a Liverpudlian he was a good mixer and possessed a sharp sense of humour, both qualities were beneficial in his new role as was a tough exterior that covered a tough interior, nobody took advantage of him or back-chatted.

Jimmy had been raised in the Dingle area of Liverpool, a district that the local constabulary never entered unless in pairs or greater numbers. He had three brothers all of whom had connections with royalty; two were residing in His Majesty's Prison Walton and the eldest was also in the Royal Navy and serving aboard HMS *Indefatigable*. He had undergone a tough childhood like most of his contemporaries, the timid and sensitive rarely survived. Despite this, Jimmy was a kindly soul at heart and fiercely loyal to those he considered his friends. He took his role as mess senior very seriously guiding and advising with infinite patience and chastising the slackers and bullies. His appearance was sufficient deter any of the recruits from trying to take advantage of him; square set, hard muscled and with a face that told of a hard life. He had the countenance of a forty-year-old pugilist on a seventeen-year-old's head, but when Jimmy smiled it was like the sun bursting forth from a thundercloud.

After being kitted out on the first day they were fully occupied from reveille at 0600 hours to lights out at 2130 hours. For the first two weeks most time was spent square bashing and performing PT, the former to instil discipline and smartness and the latter to increase their fitness. The fare in the mess was plain but nutritious and the frailer boys soon increased their body weight and stamina.

The camaraderie, unique to the services, developed quickly and competition between the messes was intense but friendly. Apart from the rivalry in training they also played organised football matches against each other on Wednesday afternoons, the time dedicated to sport in all three services. Those who preferred not to indulge in sport had the choice of working on their kit, so it was play or work.

Jack loved the PT and would have enjoyed the sessions of drill on the square had it not been for the fact that Corporal Eaton was not a forgiving soul and held Jack responsible for the heinous crime that had taken place on their first day – talking. So that now every drill session had become a nightmare and it seemed so unfair. Everybody had been subjected to ferocious disapproval for lack of effort or responding incorrectly to an order, but Jack was vilified at every drill session.

"You're bleeding idle," Eaton would scream inches from Jack's face. *Idle* covered every misdemeanour and sufficed when the transgression was in the imagination of the instructor. Movements were *idle*, turnout was *idle*, haircuts were *idle*; the staff found it a most useful word, they had no need to go into detail over the specifics of the offence, *idle* said it all.

Unfortunately for Jack, his *idleness,* on occasion, brought punishment down on the entire mess usually resulting in an extra fifteen minutes drill or being doubled around the square for ten minutes. The majority of his messmates understood what was going on and sympathised with his plight.

"He's got it in for you Jackie lad," Ronnie observed, "I don't know why yer don't complain."

"Who the bloody hell is 'e gonna complain to," Jimmy looked from the letter he was writing, "Fitz, the Commodore?"

"There must be someone," Ronnie protested.

'Yer in the Navy soft lad, not a bloody Sunday school choir," Jimmy dismissed the idea.

"The only 'fing that bothers me," Jack spat on his boot and brushed it vigorously, "is that you fellahs keep getting t' share in me punishment."

"Ay and that bothers me too, Shrimp," Buchan, a lanky Scot wandered down the mess buffing a leather belt, "I'm sick o' doing extra drill just cos' you're a useless little squirt."

"It ain't Jacks fault," Bill glared angrily at the Scot, "Eaton's always picking..."

"Shut it, Ginger," Buchan jabbed a finger in Bills direction.

"Buchan!" Jimmy interceded, "get back up the other end of the mess." It was said quietly but the menace was unmistakable and Buchan, glowering, but silent, returned to the far end of the huge hall.

"Tell you what, Jimmy," Jack said as scrubbed laundry on the floor of the washhouse one Wednesday afternoon, "I'm surprised there's no boxing."

"Boxing," Jimmy threw his soapy shirts into one of the large stone sinks and turned the tap on, "the Navy's boxing mad, in fact it's compulsory after yer fourth week," he turned off the tap, "Why, d'you fancy yerself with the gloves on Jackie?"

"I've done a bit."

"I gotta say, he is pretty handy," Bill confirmed

"Well if yers that good, they're always looking people for the matches against other Divisions and army teams..."

"D'they have a dwarf-weight?" Buchan shouted from the far end of the room as he turned the handle of the mangle;those around him laughed.

Jack slowly got to his feet, and with gritted teeth, his fists clenched and a scowl on his face, he moved towards the taunting group, but Jimmy laid a restraining arm across his chest.

"Listen mate," Jack shouted, "it ain't the size of the dog in the fight that counts, it's the size of the fight in the dog."

"Away ye wee bastard," Buchan advanced to meet him cheered on by his companions, "I could whip half a dozen puppies like you."

"I've warned you before, Buchan," Jimmy stepped between them.

"That's why he's so cocky; he's got you protecting him." Buchan sneered.

"I don't need anyone to protect me," Jack blazed.

"Punch 'im in the gob, Jack," Ronnie urged.

"He couldn't reach ma' mouth," Buchan jeered to more laughter, "even if he was standing on a chair," more laughter.

"Let me go, Jimmy," Jack wrestled to break free from Jimmy's powerful hold.

"If there's trouble I get it in the neck," Jimmy hissed.

Jack ceased his struggle, "Sorry, Jim."

Jimmy released him, "There is a way you can sort it," he said softly so that the others could not hear.

"How?"

"In the gym, that's permitted, but he's a lot bigger and heavier than you, Jack, you'd be taking a lot on."

Jack thought for a moment eyeing the tall Scot as he stood grinning at the far side of the washroom, "Yeah, well I ain't scared of him."

Buchan heard him. "Nor should ya' be wi' Cookie ta' hide behind."

Jimmy grabbed Jack as he launched himself across the room, "I've a good mind to give yer a smack meself, Buchan," and then, softly to Jack, "D'you wanna fight 'im?"

"Bloody right I do."

Jimmy surveyed the thirty or so boys at their laundry chores, all of them quiet, their arms covered in soapsuds and their working order soaking wet. All eyes were on him.

"You two," he pointed threateningly at Buchan and Jack, "stay away from each other or I'll batter the pair of yers. I'm going over to the gym to see if yer can sort this now, I'll be back in ten minutes."

After a half an hour Jimmy had returned and told the two potential adversaries to go and change into PT kit. They now stood facing each other from opposite corners of the boxing ring with a brawny PTI between them as referee. The PTI beckoned them into the middle of the ring.

"You'll fight three, three minute rounds and then shake hands whatever the outcome. That will end the bad blood between you and if it continues out of the ring you'll both be subject to naval discipline. Do you agree to that?" the two boys nodded. The PTI continued."You will step back when I say *break* and stop fighting when I say *stop,* understood?" Both nodded again. "My decision is final; any fighter that fails to leave his corner on the bell will be deemed to have lost the contest even though they may be ahead on points, okay? Right, touch gloves and go to your corners and wait for the bell."

Bill and Ronnie waited in the corner both were taking their responsibilities as his seconds seriously with towels round their necks and a bucket of water on the floor beside them.

"Just to wipe the blood away," Bill grinned.

"Shut up, Asher," Ronnie jabbed him in the ribs, "what yer trying to do to the lad, put the mockers on him?" He winked at Jack, "Yer got do well 'ere mate, I've taken a few bob on you from Buchan's pals an' there's no way I can pay up if you lose."

"Thanks, Ron," Jack gave his friend a sidelong glance of annoyance, fearful of taking his eyes of his opponent, "that's just what I need; worrying whether you get bashed after I do."

Bill patted him on his back, "You'll sort 'im, Jack," he grinned confidently.

"Yeah," Jack replied with less assurance. He studied his adversary in the brief moments before contest began and experienced a twinge apprehension. The Scot was a head taller than he was and now that he was stripped for action he did not appear quite so lanky, he was fairly well muscled and his look of complete confidence unnerved Jack a little. The words of his father, about the size of a dog in the fight, gave him some comfort.

The noise in the hall grew as other messes, hearing of the impending contest, hurried across to the witness the exchange. In a space of ten minutes over fifty boys had gathered and a half dozen of the instructors. At the sound of the bell that signified the outbreak of hostilities the noise ceased as though a switch had been thrown. This was the custom in the navy. Any amount of cheering and jeering could be created between rounds but during the actual fight complete silence was expected, and enforced.

Jack's anxiety was heightened as Buchan advanced across the ring in a crouching stance with both gloves raised in front of his upper chest; it was the poise of someone who had previous experience of the noble art. They met in the middle of the ring like two crouching gargoyles, wary, coiled and prepared to defend or attack. Buchan wasted no time in prowling, looking for a gap in his opponents defence, for he had a great reach advantage and his first jab caught Jack a glancing blow on the side of his head.It was a jab that delivered more power than any jab he had experienced in the past; it was delivered with power of a punch. Jack saw stars, he was almost stunned. Luckily, Buchan's confidence was immense and he did not feel the need to pursue his advantage, he wanted to play with his opponent, to punish him. Grinning, he danced lightly away.

As Jack tried to close in and get within range he received another two jabs to the head but they had less force than the first but sufficient to be effective and keep him at bay. Jack was worried; he had taken on an adversary with equal skill to his own but with the added benefits of reach and weight. By the end of the round Jack had only managed to land three effective body punches and he had sustained a cut on the bridge of his nose.

"Come on, Jack," Ronnie urged, "you've gotta beat 'im or I'm in up t'me ears."

"Shut up, Ronnie," Bill dabbed the cut on Jack's nose with the dampened towel.

"Well I'm worried," Ronnie moaned.

"You're bleeding worried," Jack wiped his face with the back of his glove, "it's me that's getting the thumping."

"Naw, you've got the measure 'im, Jackie lad," Ronnie sounded more concerned than convincing.

Jack blessed him with a disparaging look as the bell sounded and he stood to re-entered the fray, the story about the size of the dog in fight set firmly in his mind. Buchan left his corner with the casual air of someone setting out for a stroll, his gloves carelessly crossed over his midriff and a look of contempt on his face. Another of his father's gems of wisdom crossed his mind – the best form of defence is attack – he had nothing to lose, Buchan was going to annihilate him if he continued to conduct an orthodox fight. Surprise and attack were the order of the day. No more ducking and weaving searching for an opening through Buchan's long-range defence.

With both arms flailing viciously, Jack launched himself at his sneering adversary, his chin tucked tightly into his chest and his head down. Buchan had no defence against the sudden charge and because of the speed and suddenness of it he was unable to avoid the onslaught. Both boys fell to the canvass in a flurry of arms and legs. A great cheer went up from the onlookers contrary to the rules and it was met by shouts for silence from the staff.

The referee dragged them to their feet, "Break!" he pushed them apart.

With a surge of jubilation Jack saw that Buchan was bleeding from his nose and his lower lip was cut but the look in his eyes was murderous.

"Box on," the referee said and stepped back.

Buchan now approached the battle with a little less élan but with evident purpose. Two, rapid left jabs forced Jack's head back and were followed by swinging right to his head that sent him to the floor stunned, but before the referee could start his count Jack was back on his feet, but still dizzy from the blow.

"You alright?" the PTI stared into Jacks eyes.

Jack nodded and raised his gloves, "Yeah."

He had just steadied himself as Buchan moved in on him again; tightly defending and snaking painful jabs that forced Jack back onto the ropes where he took a number energy sapping body blows before the referee once again intervened.

"Break!"

The bell brought Jack momentary relief and as he returned to his corner he could taste blood in his mouth and as he wiped his nose with the back of his glove, it came away bloodied.

"You 'ad him going there for a minute, Jack," Ronnie looked even more worried.

"Try to stay away from him, Jack," Jimmy had joined Ronnie and Bill in the corner, "use yer feet more."

Bill wiped his face with a dampened towel, "D'you want me t' chuck the towel in, Jack?"

"No bloody way," but he wished he could have said, yes.

52

Jimmy continued with his advice, "Keep weaving, keep low, try to get under his guard. You're harder for 'im to hit if yer low."

Jack nodded conscious that his ribs ached from the last assault and his right eye was starting to close. The bell, ominously loud, silenced the cheering crowd, and the two gladiators left their respective corners for the final round.

"Touch gloves, step back and then fight on," the PTI ordered.

Buchan reversed the action from the previous round and went straight into the attack; Jack was grounded with a stunning blow to his already closing eye. As he knelt on the floor trying to regain his senses he could feel the warm blood running down the side of his cheek. The referee had reached 'six' as Jack staggered to his feet. The large PTI stood in front of him, taking both of his wrists and wiping Jacks gloves on his spotless white vest, smearing it with blood.

"D'you want to go on? I could stop it," he muttered quietly.

Jack shook his battered head, "No!"

"Box on."

Sensing that a quick ending was nigh Buchan launched another ferocious assault forcing Jack onto the ropes. Jack covered his face with his gloves and tried to duck and weave to avoid the blows that rained on his body and head. Through the haze he heard the PTI order them to 'break' and the onslaught ceased.

"D'you, want me to stop it son?" then the PTI added, "I could make you stop."

"Please, let me go on. I'm alright, honest."

A look that was a mixture of doubt and admiration crossed the PTI's rugged features. He hesitated.He nodded slightly, "Box on."

Jack met Buchan's next attack with grim determination but little effective defence and as a consequence continued to take significant punishment that resulted in the cut above his eye starting to bleed again and a another trickle of blood from his nose.

Once more his was on his knees, dazed, and shaking his head to try and clear the haze. In the distance he could hear a voice, the PTI was crouched beside him counting and marking each number with a downward motion of his hand.

"Five, six..."

Using the ropes Jack dragged himself to his feet, dashed away the blood from his eyes and adopted the stance to carry on the fight.

The referee wiped Jack gloves again, "If yer go down again I'm stopping it."

Jack shook his head, "I won't," he said, sounding as though he really believed it.

It was a lucky punch that was partly due to Buchan's eagerness to end the fight. A desperate, right uppercut delivered with all of the power that Jack could muster, caught the tall Scot squarely in the solar plexus. His advance stopped as though he had walked into an invisible wall, his eyes started and he was visibly struggling to breathe. Then, his knees buckled like a puppet that had had its strings cut and he sank with a thud to the floor, momentarily remaining in a praying position until he rolled sideways clutching his midriff and gasping for air.

The cheers drowned the referee's count and the NCOs' shouts for silence went unheeded or unheard. As the PTI's arm went down to signify the count of seven, the final bell sounded to end the contest. When Buchan had recovered, the referee's decision was that the result was a draw. This was met with howls of protest, which was quickly quietened as Fitz climbed, clumsily, into the ring.

"Dat was a good foight, so it was," he surveyed the young shining faces as though expecting dispute, "and the best decision dat there could be." He indicated the two battered adversaries with his stick, "Both boys fought wid courage and determination, and dat's what the Navy wants in its men; guts and grit. You've seen a fine example of both here today, carry dat idea wid you when yous are finished here and you join your ships to do battle wid the Hun."The CPO silently examined the eager young faces wondering how many would live to manhood. "I t'ink three cheers would be the roight thing, Staff." With that he left the ring with the same lack of dexterity that he had entered it.The PTI led the spectators in a rousing three cheers for the two fighters, after which they were made to shake hands to signify the end of their feud.

As Fitz passed Corporal Eaton, he muttered, "Young Cornwell's a plucky little bugger, so he is."

"That's a fact, Sir," was the reply.

From that day forth Jack's time spent on the drill square bore no more horror. Jacks lot improved immensely from then on in every respect and he really began to enjoy all off his training, life was looking good. But at the beginning of October sadness invaded his euphoria: he received a desperate letter from Romin informing him that Clive had been wounded in the Battle of Loos and John Kipling was reported missing, believed killed.

Chapter Six

Captain's rounds took place every Saturday morning and it was an event that involved all ranks in a great amount of scrubbing, polishing, ironing and most all anxiety. The recruits worried, and those supervising them worried. The slightest hint of rust, the smallest speck of dust or an item of kit imprecisely placed, could result in all liberty being curtailed and extra duties or fatigues to even those only vaguely connected to the gross breach of negligence.

The Captain was bad enough but what made the inspection worse was the fact that he was accompanied by CPO Fitzgerald. The Captain had been known not to spot that a sailor's spare bootlaces had not been rolled to precisely a two-inch diameter, or a minusculespeck of cotton besmirched a ratings blue serge jacket. Fitz missed nothing, and the misdemeanours overlooked by the Captain he used to recruit a small gathering of 'volunteers' for tasks that that did not really come under normal naval jurisdiction.

So it was, on Saturday November the first. The Captain and his entourage had passed Jack and Bill by without adverse comment, and young Lieutenant Tetlow had even praised Jack for the standard of his kit layout, but Fitz, following on behind, saw things a little differently.

"Oi'll see you two in my office at noon," he paused and looked a little longer at their pristine accoutrements, "Disgusting!"He turned his squinty gaze at Jimmy, "Dese 'ere two reprobates are on your watch, aren't they Cook?"

Jimmy snapped to attention, "Aye, Sir."

"Roight, you report wid them."

"Aye aye,Sir."

56

At twelve the three of them stood in a line against the wall outside the CPO's office waiting tentatively, and mystified as to their offences.

"You two 'ave dropped me in it," Jimmy muttered out of the corner of his mouth.

"But I don't know what we've done," Jack replied with equal caution.

"He said you were, disgusting." Jimmy reminded them.

"That's just Fitz..."

"Hey up, he's here," the three of them came to attention as the tall Ulsterman came striding along the corridor.

"Inside," he ordered. "Roight," he said when they were neatly lined in front of his desk, "dat was a bloody poor turnout, so it was." Fitz was not showing any anger; in fact his normal leer had almost turned into a smile, "but I'm going to be lenient wid yer as Christmas is not too far away."

Jimmy was beginning to consider if he preferred Fitz when he was going puce with rage, for everyone in the barracks knew that his ranting and ravings were mainly an act to intimidate the recruits.

He continued, "So your punishment is going have a bit o' fun attached," he paused enjoying the looks of puzzlement and distrust,"you'll go straight to the gymnasium after mess call and report to the wife of Commander Fordham."

Jimmy was tempted to ask why but knew better, "Aye aye, Sir."

Throughout their meal they pondered on their mysterious fate, their assumptions punctuated by threats from Jimmy.

"You sods 'ave dropped me in it," he moaned as he spread jam on a thick slice of bread, "if this is a rotten job we've got, I'll give yer both a smack."

"Come on Jimmy," Jack protested, "you know he picks people out for jobs 'e wants doing, with no good reason."

"Yeah," Bill agreed, "you told us that when we first joined."

"Well if it's a rotten job you'll still get smacked." Jimmy replied.

*

Mrs Fordham was a formidable lady of sturdy stature with a voice like a sergeant major and a persona that invited neither question nor disagreement.

"Come in boys, come in," she commanded from her position by the piano that had been placed at the far end of the gym, "don't be shy."

A score or so ratings gathered to one side of the piano looking decidedly ill at ease, a few carried musical instruments and one, a ventriloquists dummy dressed in naval uniform.

"Are you volunteers?" Mrs. Fordham enquired.

"Chief Fitzpatrick sent us Ma'am." Jimmy explained.

"Ah, you're the 'three little maids,'" she beamed. "Madeline, Madeline," she called, "where is that girl?"

A pretty girl with short blonde curls and boyish figure emerged from a side room carrying some brightly coloured garments.

"Yes, Mother."

"Madeline dear, these are our little maids," Mrs Fordham gushed, "take them away and find kimonos to fit them."

"What's all this about?" Jimmy asked of Madeline when she had taken them into a small room.

"You don't know," she looked genuinely surprised and equally amused.The three bewildered young sailors shook their heads anxiously."But I thought that you had volunteered to do the little maids song from the Mikado."

58

Again three heads shook and they exchanged nervous looks."What's Mikado?" Jimmy asked.

"And we didn't volunteer for anyfing," Bill added.

Madeline was finding the situation getting funnier by the minute, "It's an operetta by Gilbert and Sullivan."

"And who's the little maids?" Jack asked fearing the worst.

"Well it rather looks as though you are," Madeline replied. "They are three Japanese schoolgirls and..."

"Japanese schoolgirls!" the despair and horror was in unison.

"No bloody way," Jimmy headed for the door where he almost collided with CPO Fitzgerald.

"And where moight you be going, Cook?"

"Er...er...I...I think there's been some sort of mistake, Sir," he stammered.

"And why would you be thinking dat?" He watched Jimmy with a smirk on his face and his eyes half closed.

"Well, they...this young lady," he began, "seems to think that we," he waved a hand to encompass Jack and Bill, "are going to do an opera or something."

"Oh, dear me no, there's been no mistake laddie, but don't you be worrying about having to sing an opera; it's just one little song. Now I t'ink Miss Fordham was measuring yous for your dresses and then Mrs Fordham is going to run you through the little ditty." He turned to leave but stopped at the door to add the coup de grace, "and the little dance."

After two hours of their first rehearsal for their part in the camps Christmas concert, the three of them made their way back to the mess in differing moods. Jimmy was in shock. The thought of performing in front of the whole complement of HMS *Vivid*, dressed as a female and singing and dancing was enough to make him consider suicide or desertion. To make matters worse, the other two members of the trio had eventually found the whole affair a bit of a lark and were playing on Jimmy's discomfiture, but not too much.

After they had sung the song, Three Little Maids from School, through a few times, Mrs Fordham tried to get it sounding a little more feminine.

"That's very good so far boys, but let's try again but this time with falsetto."

"What's she talking about?" Jimmy muttered out of the corner of his mouth.

"Sing like a girl," Bill hissed, grinning.

The look of shock that Jimmy had worn since being fitted for his kimono escalated into one of panic.

"I can't sing like a bloody girl," his urgent whisper was obviously audible to Mrs Fordham.

"There is no such word as 'can't' in the Royal Navy," she rapped the piano with the pencil that she had been using as a conductors baton, "what's your name?"

"Cook, Ma'am."

"Cook, I would advise that you refrain from coarse language. Now, let us try again," she nodded at the pianist and the strains of the jocular tune filled the hall, with Jack and Bill producing acceptable falsetto and Jimmy still sounding like gravel being poured onto a sheet of corrugated iron.

"Three little maids from school are we, pert as school-girls well can be..."

Mrs Fordham gritted her teeth and closed her eyes, while behind her Madeline hid her face in her hands, her body shaking with suppressed laughter.

"If you two let this get out," Jimmy warned as they headed back to their mess, "I'll bloody kill yer."

"But everyone's gonna know in the end," Jack pulled a face and shrugged.

Jimmy stopped and face his fellow 'maids,' "I know that, clever, but they'll only be able to take the Mickey for a couple of days after the concert cos' we'll being going on Christmas leave; but if they find out now we'll 'ave weeks of hell."

*

Throughout the rest of November and the first two weeks of December, they had to attend rehearsals every Wednesday and Sunday evening. These clandestine visits to the gymnasium were accounted for, to the rest of the mess, by the three of them donning PT kit on the pretence that they were training for the end of term cross-countrysteeplechase.

Mrs Fordham had acquiesced and allowed them to rehearse in a spare room. Luckily, none of the other acts came from their mess so their secret was maintained; though Jimmy lived in constant fear that the dreadful news would be made public before the concert.

The night of the concert produced a great deal of excitement for the whole barracks,for not only was it an auspicious occasion in itself, but the following day the majority of the staff and all of the recruits were to embark on Christmas leave.The absence of Jimmy, Bill and Jack from the audience was commented on by a number of their messmates, but the thrill of the event quickly suppressed their curiosity.As the lights in the body of the hall dimmed, the gaslights along the foot of the stage brightened, the hubbub of noise dwindled to a hushed, tense expectancy.

The first act was Leading Hand Pennel, a ventriloquist of limited talent, whose lips moved more noticeably than the dummies. He was followed by a magician with even less aptitude, who ended his disastrous but hilarious act by attempting to make a pigeon disappear and spent the rest of the evening trying to coax the frightened bird down from the rafters.

Next came the Chaplain who received polite applause for his rendering of Kipling's *If* and *The Charge of the Light Brigade* byAlfred Lord Tennyson. A more enthusiastic welcome was givento Miss Madeline Fordham for her rendition of a Marie Lloyd song; *The Boy I Love is up in the Gallery*.The master of ceremonies, a rotund petty officer, had great difficulty bringing the applause to an end.

"And now messmates," he bellowed, when silence eventually reigned, "we have a special treat from the mystic East." He paused for a murmur of excited anticipation. "For your delight we have three, beautiful, Japanese maids to please and entertain you." With a raised arm of introduction he moved to the side of the stage as the pianist played the bouncy chords of the introduction.

The curtains opened to reveal three 'females' at the back the stage attired in brightly coloured kimonos, jet-black hair piled high and exotically decorated fans covering their faces. The guttering gaslight, make up and distance, disguised the 'maids' identity and true gender. In time with the jaunty tune they shuffled to the front of the stage in a gait that resembled the movement of geisha's, their stride restricted by their tight garments, short mincing steps and fanning themselves as they progressed.

Gradually laughter replaced the silent awe when the 'maids' began to sing, the audience gradually realised that the three 'maids' were anything but;

*"Three little maids from school are we, pert as a school-girl well can be, filled to the brim with girlish glee."*The dance steps were simple; twelve short steps to the front of the stage, then eight towards the right wing, turn and sixteen to the left, all the time fanning themselves and trying to look coy. Laughter gradually died away as disbelief and anticipation spread through the audience.

"It's Cookie," a voice bellowed above the tinkling piano and trilling trio. Not even in a poorly contrived falsetto could Jimmy's grating Liverpudlian accent be concealed.

Jimmy had gained some comfort that none of his messmates knew of his part in the concert, and he even believed that with all of the makeup, wig, and use of the fan, his dreadful secret could be preserved. Now the truth was out, the thought of the mockery that would now be inevitable and the predictable violence that would ensue filled him with horror, but worse, it affected his concentration.

The shout of recognition came just as they turned to retrace their steps across the stage but Jimmy, distracted, was not counting, and as the other two turned to go stage left he was still continuing stage right. In the collision with Bill his wig slipped sideways, precariously held from falling off completely by pins but giving him the appearance of a drunken fishwife. As they moved in such close proximity it was crucial that they were in step, but this discipline also failed in the confusion.

Jimmy's attentionhad completely gone, thrown by the awfulness of his situation. The worldly-wise Scouser, confident and comfortable with his lot, had been replaced by a dithering incompetent who had lost complete control of both his mind and body. As Jimmy shuffled to regain the step, Jack, inadvertently, trod firmly on his kimono. The exposure of white hairy legs raised the roof and ribald catcalls and wolf whistles obliged some of the senior ratings to try and restore order. It took some time.

"Show us yer legs Cookie,"

"Yer can share my 'ammock anytime dearie,"

"See yer after the show sweetie," were but a few of the more decorous comments hurled at the 'girls' before calm could be reinstated.

Throughout this maelstrom the 'maids' had endeavoured, manfully, to complete their dance routine. The song, however, was not only pointless because of the din, but also impossible as Jimmy cursed his two dancing partners for causing his demise by their clumsiness.

"Pair of bloody oafs," he snarled as he steadied his wig with one hand and tried to restore his modesty with the other.

"Oafs!" Jack squealed still maintaining falsetto, "it was your bleeding fault."

"Turn!" Bill said urgently, "turn, turn."

They shuffled back across the stage fanning themselves and two of them offering sickly smiles to the audience while Jimmy continued to utter dire threats, still clutching his kimono and supporting his wayward wig.

"Sing, sing." Bill urged as a resemblance of peace fell upon the gathering.

Bill led the way and the other two picked up the line, hesitantly, "..*Come from a ladies seminary, freed from its tutelary, three little maids from school, three little maids from school.*"

As the song ended they thankfullyreached the wings and disappeared from view to a roar of appreciation from the gathered complement of *Vivid*.

"Go back, go back," a stern Mrs Fordham ushered them back onto the stage, "take a bow."

Bill and Jack, still respectably attired and grinning, revelled in the adulation while Jimmy, looking like a dishevelled tart, scowled and made perfunctory bows as he unceasingly muttered dreadful threats at his fellow entertainers, while in the wings Mrs Fordham admonished her daughter and other back stage staff for their lack of professionalism as they shared in the mirth of the audience.

"Curtains, curtains," she herded Able Seaman Gilbert to his post.

"It could 'ave been good," Jack bemoaned as they left the stage.

"It was his fault," Bill thrust a thumb at Jimmy, "he can't count."

"You knocked me bloody wig off, this silly bugger stood on me dress," Jimmy defended himself angrily, "and your blaming that cock-up on me."

"If you 'ad been counting yer steps," Bill jabbed a finger with equal anger, "I wouldn't have bumped into ya."

"Boys, boys," Madeline stepped between them, "shhh, you'll be heard," she indicated a grey haired three striper sat on a chair centre stage preparing to play a large accordion.

"Fitz'll 'ave our guts for garters," Jimmy hissed, "we'll be on punishment for the rest of our bleeding service."

Jimmy had underestimated his standing at *Vivid*, and apart from grins of appreciation and the odd 'great show,' no mockery was made of their part in the concert. There was no reason to call on his ability with his fists that he had demonstrated at the last inter-ship boxing contest and as the following day progressed so his mood improved. His frame of mind took a turn for the worse when a Writer came into the mess at the end of the days training.

"Cook," he called from the door.

Jimmy raised a hand, "Here!"

"Report to Chief Fitzgerald."

"What for?"

"Just do it," the Writer departed.

Jimmy picked up his cap, "Miserable sod," he paused at the door,"if this is about last night and I'm in the brown stuff, you two better leave the country," he pointed a threatening finger at Bill and Jack.

Fifteen minutes later he returned ebullient, "I've gotta ship," he threw his cap in the air, "and," he tapped the side of his nose, "the Chief thinks I made the show and you two turbots were just 'angers on'."

"Bloody cheek," Jack shook his head smiling, "you made a right pigs ear…"

"Not according to the Chief," Jimmy grinned.

"So what ship have you got?" Bill asked

"HMS *Birkenhead*, she'll be commissioned in April with HMS *Chester*."

"When d'you join her?" Jack was disappointed that they were losing Jimmy.

"Straight from Christmas leave, I've got me travel warrant to Birkenhead; she's been built at Cammell Lairdand that's where I join her, so I'll be able to get some time at home in Liverpool."

"Who'll take over from you, here?" Jack asked, his worry deepening.

"What, nurse-maiding you lot?"

"Yeah!"

"You don't have anyone in your second term; they reckon you should know the drill by then."

Chapter Seven

With little free time to be wasteful with, the first three months of their training had sped past. Christmas was upon them, and with it their first leave home, the excitement level was high.

"It'll be bedlam at the station," Jimmy had warned them, "the entire Andrew stationed in Plymouth will be trying to get home."

"I thought they put on special trains?"Jack asked.

"They do," Jimmy assured them, "but it's still everyman for himself; you'll be lucky to get a seat," he tied the rope at the neck of his sailor's bag, "I've got to go and get my joining orders from the Division office, so you get down to the station and save me a seat."

"We won't be going on the same train as you," Bill pointed out, "we're going to London."

"So am I," Jimmy heaved his bag onto his shoulder, "it's quicker going via Euston."

As Jimmy left Ronnie entered the mess carrying his laundry and a bar of carbolic soap.

"Rum time to be doing yer wash,Ron," Jack said, "Jimmy said we should get down the station rapid, cos it'll be crowded.

Ronnie dumped his kit onto his sailors box, "I ain't going anywhere," he kept his back to them.

"What! You ain't going home for Christmas?"

"I ain't got a 'ome Jack, I'm an orphan, remember." He turned to face them, his eyes moist and a look shame and embarrassment on his thin face.

"Garn, you ain't staying here on yer own." Bill looked determined.

"I won't be on me own,"Ronnie explained, "there'll be lots of chaps on duties and..."

"No matter," Bill took charge much to Jack's relief and surprise, "Jack will pack some kit for yer,

67

and you and me will go down to the Div office to get your leave pass and warrant; you can stay with us."

"But I can't just turn up, your mum might..."Ronnie began.

"I guarantee my mum will welcome you like family. Now come on."

Jack felt inclined to mention that this could possibly make them late for their train, and there may be no staff in the office, but the selfishness of the thought made him hold his silence.Bill's positive action got the results that they wanted much to everybody's surprise, including Bill's. The clerk had proved cooperative and had sought out the orderly officer who was also agreeable to what was required, and he had signed both the leave pass and travel warrant.

Red faced and sweating, despite the coldness of the day, they arrived at the station and forced their way through the navy blue throng to platform four where the Paddington train stood; filling rapidly. Ronnie, being less laden than the other two, found a compartment occupied by only four people. The boys piled their kit onto the luggage racks and took their seats, breathless and happy.

"We'd better put some kit on that seat to save it for Jimmy," Jack suggested, indicating one of the two remaining seats.

Maurice Hindle was a bully, of that there was no question. He had been on the permanent staff at HMS *Vivid* since his enlistment two years earlier and had somehow evaded being posted to a ship during that period; nor had he sought such a posting. Maurice was happy in his stores and he had every intention of staying there as long as he could. His position of comfort in his current posting and his renown for bad behaviour were tolerated by those in command because of his prowess as a boxer.He had only been beaten once in the last two years and was considered an important asset to the boxing team.

His appearance matched his character perfectly. A thick thatch of, darkly blonde hair, sat above a low forehead and small close-set eyes like a pile of mouldy hay. He was broad shouldered and thick set with heavy, but not well defined, muscles. Maurice was a northerner, from Wigan, and was the sort of northerner that gets those who hail from that beautiful county of Lancashire, a bad name.

Just as Jack, Bill and Ronnie had settled into their seats, full of excitement and seasonal spirit, Maurice climbed into the compartment with two, equally distasteful companions.

"There's room in 'ere lads," he pointed to the bag that Jack had placed on the seat, "whose is that?"

"We're saving a seat for a mate." Bill explained.

"Ay, well I'm yer mate, thanks," he threw the bag onto the floor.

"Hey!" Jack jumped to his feet, "you can't do that."

Maurice look down at Jack who barely came up to his chin, "You what? Who's gonna stop me," he grinned wickedly, "you?" He shoved Jack in the chest, hard enough to push him back into his seat. "Right, cos it's Christmas I'm not gonna batter you but because you've been a cheeky little sod tha' can't stay in my compartment. Which is your kit?" He eyed the items stowed on the luggage rack.

Jack was back on his feet, his eyes full of defiance, "I ain't telling yer."

Maurice threw his head back in mock horror."Somebody tell this cheeky little sod who I am."

"I know who you are, Maurice," Jimmy forced his way into the compartment past Maurice's friends who crowded the door enjoying the baiting, "an' you're not very nice."

Maurice turned to face the intruder, "Ah, Cookie lad, not wearing your dress today, then?"

69

Jimmy stood with his face inches from Hindle's, "Wouldn't matter if I was wearing a bloody dress or a nappy, I could still take you, Maurice."

Jack, like the rest of them had seen Jimmy angry in the past when they had been slacking or larking about. But the look he saw on Jimmy's rugged face now, truly frightened him, he was looking at a dangerous man. His heavy jaw was set and his half-closed eyes, hard and without a hint of mercy in them.

Maurice seemed undaunted by Jimmy's demeanour but Jack suspected a trace uncertainty in his voice when he spoke.

"I've only been beaten once Cookie and you were lucky then."

Jimmy's granite face gave the impression of hardening even more, "That was Queensbury Rules, Maurice."

There was a brief flurry of almost undetectable movement and Maurice's eyes started from his head; he emitted a long hiss of breath which gradually changed to a moanof pain as he slowly sank to his knees, his hands clutching his groin.

Jimmy looked down at him, his face devoid of any pity, "These are Liverpool rules Maurice," he said quietly, and then delivered a mighty punch to the side of his helpless adversary's jaw, rendering him senseless.

"Get 'im off," he ordered Maurice's companions, who stood by dumfounded.

As the limp form of *Vivid*'s bully was dragged onto the platform the guards whistle shrilled and theengine screeched in reply, the last of the doors slammed and the train jolted into motion.

"You'll be sorry for this, Cook," one of Maurice's attendants bawled safely from the platform as the train eased slowly forward.

"Gosh, Jimmy," was all Jack could say as he sank back into his seat, "thanks for that, I thought I was gonna get marmalized."

"He's a bad bugger,"Jimmy replied nonchalantly as he stowed his kit and then dropped heavily into his seat grinning, "but he's no trouble now."

"But what about when we go back?" Bill asked worriedly.

"Have you ever seen 'im before?" All three shook their heads, "Well then, it's not likely you'll see him again, it's a big base and he won't know which division you're in."

"Yeah, all the same..."

"Bill, don't worry about him," Jimmy grinned, "I'm the one he'd want, if he had the guts."

"Yeah but you'll 'ave gone on posting,"Ronnie pointed out.

"Enjoy yer leave and forget 'im," Jimmy dismissed their fears with a wave of his hand.

*

The kitchen was warm and welcoming; it smelt of Christmas, spices and the pine of the Christmas tree mingled with the aroma of freshly baked mince pies and Christmas cake. The ceiling was brightly decorated with homemade paper chains and sprigs of holly protruded from behind picture frames and the large mirror over the sideboard. Lily was alone and working at the range with her back to the room.On the table were bowls filled with cooked fruit and a pile of dough was resting on a plate. Lily carried out all of her chores with great vitality and this usually involved a fair degree of noise especially when she was cooking.

Jack made no sound; he stood soaking up the homeliness, feeling a little emotional and suddenly aware that he had been suffering from homesickness all these past months, but had been too busy to realise it. Now he had a full week's leave, a week to wallow in idleness and self-gratification. No parades, no PT, no drill, no inspection or endless fatigues.

"Well 'ow about a nice mug of tea then?"

Lily gave a screech of shock and turned to face the intruder, "You little sod. How long have you been standing there?" Without waiting for a reply she enveloped her grinning son to her ample chest and then stood back holding him at arm's length. "Look at you," her eyes filled and she shook her head, "look at you, a sailor. Where's my little Jackie gone?"

"Cut it out,Mum," Jack felt himself filling up, "what did you expect?" He kissed the top of her head."Where is everyone?"

"Lil's just popped out to take cards to her friends;" she explained, "George has gone on an errand for old Mrs Potter, Maud's still at work..."

"What about Dad?" he interrupted.

"He'll be home later this evening but of course Arthur's in France and 'e won't..."she was cut short by the yard door bursting open and Lil charged into the kitchen red cheeked with the cold and exertion.

She threw her arms around Jack's waist, "Oh Jack, Jack," she began to sob, "I didn't think you'd come."

"Don't be daft; you knew I was coming home for Christmas."

"I've bad dreams about you," she managed between sobs.

"You've never told me that," Lily looked alarmed.

"What sort of dreams?" Jack seated himself and sat her on his lap.

"I dream that you're all on your own and scared," she wiped her cheeks with her hair and sniffed.

"How can I be on me own?" Jack felt the hairs on the back of his neck stand up and a shiver ran down his spine, "I've got all of me mates haven't I. Anyway,

72

what 'appens in these dreams of yours?" he asked hoping that his apprehension did not show.

She sniffed again and shook her head, "It's all a bit mixed up," she began, "there's a lot of noise and fires, and your all on your own and your frightened but trying not to be..." the tears began to flow down her cheeks and she looked deeply into his eyes, "and I'm trying to pull you away but you won't come."

Jack's laugh was without real mirth, "And where are we when all this is going on?"

"It's a bit like a shed or some sort of building but the walls are missing."

He laughed again, "Well there you are then, nothing to worry about, sailors don't go into sheds or buildings, we're on ships all the time aren't we."

Lil did not look convinced but the arrival of George and Maud brought the eerie conversation to an end. Lily went back to her festive preparations a subdued and frightenedmother.

*

The journey across London was always an interesting event but on Christmas Eve it was doubly so. It was the second Christmas of the war and the restraints that had been the order of the first, had been cast aside, and the rationing that would be in place in the years to come was still unknown in 1915. The shop lights gave off an air of fairyland and the bustle of people doing their last minute shopping created an atmosphere of pleasurable anticipation and warmth.

Throngs of soldiers and sailors filled the streets and trams, grateful that they were the lucky ones at home for the festival. All of them were treated with affection and respect.By the time Jack reached Sikkim Hall he had been kissed by fourteen females ranging from grandmothers to schoolgirls and he had lost count of the times his hand had been shaken. He had to constantly refuse enthusiastic offers to be taken to the closest hostelry to have his health drunk.

It was dark by the time he arrived at Sikkim Hall and the seasonal celebrations did not appear to be taking place as in the rest of the city, it was almost in darkness. One bedroom window was lit and one of the main rooms on the ground floor; the light casting a delicate glow across the frosted lawn. His visit had been arranged by letter and when he knocked nervously on the kitchen door it was opened instantly by Megan, her face serious.

"Come in Jack," she kissed him lightly on the cheek.

"Is something the matter," her seriousness alarmed him, "Nobby's alright isn't he?"

"He is love, thank you for asking. Miss Romin is in Cook's parlour but you won't be able to stay long, the family are going out to dinner."

Romin was sitting by the fire and appeared to be asleep. He had forgotten how beautiful she was and was surprised how fragile she looked; she seemed to have lost weight. He coughed softly and she opened her eyes, the sad shadow left her and her face lit up with a smile.

"Jack," she jumped to her feet and hugged him, "it is so nice to see you. I'm sorry that you've had to leave your family on Christmas Eve."

He waved her protest aside, "I wouldn't 'ave missed seeing you, you know that. Is everything alright? The house seems sad."

She nodded, "Is it that apparent?"

"It is. What's the matter? Is itJohn or Clive?"

She sighed deeply and the aura of sadness settled on her once more, "Both, John is still missing and Clive's wounds are more serious than we first thought."

"Is he home, in Blighty?"

"No, he's the military hospital at Le Havre; his wounds are so serious that they dare not move him," tears filled her eyes.

Jack took her hand, "Crickey, I am sorry, an' John's still missing," it felt strange to be using officers Christian names.

She sighed again, "Yes and presumed dead, but poor Mr Kipling cannot accept it, he is insisting that there has been a mistake and the search for him should continue. He has even written to the German Embassy in America seeking their assistance, the poor man." she took his hand and led him to the sofa and they sat side by side, touching,"Jack this war is so terrible, and so many families are losing their loved ones, both here and in Germany, what is the point of all this sorrow."

Jack knew he should reply with care,"We have to beat the Hun," was the best that he could manage. He did not want her to move away, he wanted the moment to last. She felt so fragile, the confidence that arose from her breeding, position and wealth had evaporated, and she now seemed vulnerable, exposed as she now was to the true horror of the war.

She half turned to face him,"Look at you, all smart in your uniform, eager to do your bit, and here am I a pathetic civilian bemoaning the fact that the war has touched my family. Until this happened I was as jingoistic as the rest, not giving a thought for those who had already been affected." She raised his hand to her lips and kissed it, "I tell you this, Jack Cornwell, in the future I will have as much respect for the mothers and wives who have lost their loved ones as I do for you brave lads who defend us. Their courage and fortitude are magnificent." She sighed deeply and forced her smile closer too gaiety, "But I am being selfish, we don't have long, tell me how things are with you? Your letters are wonderful but you must have much more to tell me."

A light knock on the door stopped further conversation, Megan entered, smiling, with a plate of mince pies and a jug of ginger beer."Cook thought you might like these," she placed them on the table and glanced at the clock on the mantelpiece. "You'll have to be ready by half seven, Miss Romin."

"Yes, thank you, Megan."

"Me letters aren't causing a problem are they?" he asked when Megan had left.

"No, Megan's very discreet..."

The door flew open again and Megan reappeared looking flushed and anxious, "Quickly!" she beckoned Romin, "Miss Violet has been in the kitchen looking for you. You mustn't be found here, Cook would get the sack."

The look of desolation that had tainted Romin's beauty was suddenly replaced by an expression of alarm but she remained composed, "I am sorry that we have to part so suddenly, Jack," she took his hand as they left the room and they went quickly down the corridor to the kitchen where she took small package from behind a pile of crockery; it was wrapped in colourful paper. "A little gift, Happy Christmas," she kissed him on his cheek.

Flushing, at this public display of affection, he pulled a small box from the inside pocket of his tunic and handed it to her, "It ain't much, but we don't get much chance to go to shops."

"Whatever it is I shall cherish it," she kissed him again.

*

It was a crisp Christmas morning and St Michaels Church was packed to the door. The old adage; 'God and soldier, men alike adore, when in danger but not before', was proven. Jack and his father sat side by side clad in their respective khaki and navy serge, happy, with their family and friends around them and proud of their membership of His Majesty's armed forces. The only blot on the Cornwell's happiness wasArthur's absence. But still there was a measure of contentment on those present and the Spirit of Christmas washed over the congregation pushing away the fears and worries that touched every family in the land.

"There's Amy," Lil called as they left the church and she rushed across the road to the Ashton family, resplendent in an assortment of uniforms; Amy in that of the Band of Hope, Bill and Ronnie in naval and the parents in Salvation Army attire. The families exchanged seasonal greetings, the adults chatting briefly, rubbing their hands and stamping their feet to reducethe effects of the cold.

"What's all this I've been 'earing about you Cornwell?"Ronnie winkedmeaningfully and grinned.

"I dunnoRon, what you been hearing about me?" Jack was conscious that Amy was watching him keenly. They stood a little apart from their parents.

Ronnie nudged him and winked again, "Amy tells me you've got some rich girlfriend, you kept that quiet at *Vivid*, you crafty dog"

"You don't wanna believe everyfing you're told Ronnie," he threw a withering look at Amy and felt himself starting to blush.

Amy sniffed one of her disdainful sniffs, "You certainly seemed besotted at the presentation, Jack;you couldn't take your eyes of her."and she gave an equally contemptuous toss of her copper curls.

"You're just jealous," Bill poked his sister in the ribs with his elbow and she winced with pain and glared at him.

"Come on, Ronnie, its cold," she took his hand, "we'll go on ahead,Mother," she called, "and put the vegetables on," she turned to Jack. "Shall you come round this evening as normal or will you be going to visit her ladyship?"

"Yeah," Jack replied with similar scorn, "I'll be round to see Ronnie and Bill."

Ronnie grinned and winked as he was dragged away from the group.

*

The Carr-Langton's returned from churchunder a cloud of despondency over the plight of their son and heir. They shared time round the Christmas tree opening their presents as was their custom but there was little laughter, the Christmas spirit was somewhat diluted.

As soon as she considered it prudent Romin had retired to her room where she tenderly removed the scarlet wrapping paper and opened the small cardboard box that bore Jacks gift to her. Under a layer of cotton wool she found an enamel brooch of a sailor performing the hornpipe. She giggled out loud, with delight and humour, as she had done when she had received his letter telling her that he had periods of training for the hornpipe.She had seen sailors perform it once when her father had taken her to the launching of The Royal Oak.

"It was delightfully comic and very spine-tingling," she had written in response to his letter.

She kissed the brooch, "I shall always treasure you. My first gift from Jack..."

"To whom are you talking?" Violet was standing in the open door; she crossed the room to where Romin sat on her bed,"What have you got there?" she demanded.

"A present..." Romin began but before she complete the sentence Violet had snatched the brooch from her hand.

She examined it briefly and a triumphant sneer spread across her face, "I can guess who sent this," she avoided Romin's attempt to grab the doll back. "I have suspected for some time that there has been some form of communication between the two of you," she turned and headed for the door, "wait till Mother hears about this."

She had not gone more than a couple of paces when Romin, her eyes blazing, launched herself from the bed and onto her sister's back, knocking her to the ground.

"Give that back," she hissed through clenched teeth, "that's a gift from a friend." She was surprised at her own strength and with less effort than she had anticipated she yanked it from Violets hand. By now she found herself sat astride her sister but Violet had not given up the fight and she struggled to regain possession of the brooch from Romin's grasp.

"Girls, girls what on earth is going on?" Their father's appearance in the doorway brought an end to the mêlée and the two flushed and breathless girls got sheepishly to their feet. Both began speaking together and Sir James held up his hand for silence

"I am relieved that your mother or the servants were not witness to such unladylike behaviour; explain yourselves."

Again, they both started to talk but Sir James raised hand silenced them once more."As this is your room, Romin, let me hear what you have to say about this disgraceful exhibition."

Romin hung her head, "I am so sorry Father, but Violet came in and took a present from methat..."

"It came from that, awful, little working class..."

"Violet!" the anger on her father's face was sufficient to silence her,"Go on Romin."

"What is awful about Jack? You don't even know him," she glared at her sister.

"You are testing my patience, young lady," Sir James said sternly.

"Sorry Father," Romin was thankful that it had not been their mother who had witnessed what had just taken place. She went on to relate the events to her father.

"Do you disagree with what Romin has told me, Violet?" Violet shook her head but remained silent."Then why did I have to witness my daughters behaving like drunken fishwives?"

"She is consorting with a working class boy, Father, with no thought to the family's good name."

Sir James laughed shortly, "Receiving a small gift could hardly be regarded as consorting. Is this the young man who pulled you from the drainage ditch?" he asked, Romin nodded,"Leave us, if you please, Violet," Violet made to object,"do as I say," he snapped, and before she reached the door he added, "and not a word of these shockingproceedings to your mother. Do you understand?"

"Yes, Father," a subdued, and less than haughty, Violet left the room closing the door behind her.

"Now,"Sir James sat on the bed beside his daughter and put a comforting arm around her shoulder, "what is this all about."Her father smelt of cigars, brandy and cologne, and againRomin was grateful that it had been he and not her mother that she had to confess too.

She kept her head bowed and concentrated on the brooch in her hands, "We have exchanged letters Father and he came here last evening to bring me this."

Sir James took the brooch and smiled, "Has he completed his training yet?"

"No, not until April."

"It is an impossible situation my dear, you understand that?" she nodded slightly, "Your positions are poles apart and it would be difficult for you to mix comfortably with his friends or he with yours," he was silent for a few moments and, at first, Romin did not think it appropriate to offer any opinion but then decided she should.

"Clive has grown to love his men despite the gap you speak of, Father. He says that after the war he will remain friends with those he commands regardless of..."

"I know your brothers opinion on these matters," he cut in, "and I am sure there will be incalculable changes and things will never be as they were, but I am sure that the classes will still remain at some distance from each other, wealth alone will ensure this."

"But will it stop us having friends among those less fortunate?"

He took her hand, "I see no harm in your continuing to write to Jack, after all he has risked his life for you once already and he will be doing so for us all come May.

Romin stood and put her arms round her father's neck and buried her face in his neck, "Thank you Daddy."

Sir James felt a warm tear on the side of his face. He kissed the top of her head, "Come, come, there is no need to get upset. May I enquire how you two managed to communicate without it coming to your mother's attention?"Romin hesitated, Sir James continued, "am I correct in assuming that there has been some collusion with a member of staff?"

"Oh Daddy, please, I forced them," she was desperate, "please don't discharge anybody."

"There, there," he patted her back, "I won't pretend that I am pleased with what they have done but I do realise that you can be a very manipulative little monkey. You always have been since you were a small child. Was it Megan?" Romin nodded, still a little fearful, "well you have my blessing to write directly to Jack and he to you."

"What about Mother?"

"You may safely leave your mother to me."

Romin threw her arms round his neck again, "I should have known that you would understand."

Sir James smiled and tweaked her nose, "And I would like you to wear your new brooch whenever you wish," as he turned to leave the room his heart sank once more at the thought of his son, wounded, and possibly dying in a military hospital in France. He made the decision that the day following Boxing Day he would cross the Channel to see his first born, and nothing would stand in his way.

*

Jack took his sister Lil round to the Asher's just as darkness was falling. The air was cold and the cobbled street varnishedwith ice. They laughed at their drunken like stagger as they strove to remain on their feet. Giggling, Lil clutched his jersey for support, but thus hampered, Jack constantly fell, invariably with Lil on top of him.Lights from the house windows threw puddles of yellow welcoming light across the frosty pavement and the sound of laughter and music filled the wintry air with the joy of Christmas. Jack felt a sudden cloak of melancholy descend upon him and the thought that this could possibly be his last Christmas, his laughter stopped. He knelt and took his little sister in his arms and hugged her to his body.

"You're hurting me, Jack," she squealed, breathless, "what's the matter."

He released her and shook his head, glad that in the dark she could not see his tears, "Nothing, luv.Come on."

They spent two hours with Bill and his family, much as they had done for the past few years; playing games, singing carols and enjoying the wonderful spread of Christmas fare set out on the parlour table.Amy was not on her best behaviour, embarrassing both Ronnie and Jack by paying too much attention to the former in her attempt to kindle jealousy in the latter. Her antics were not in the least subtle, even Lil was aware of something amiss.

"Why is Amy being 'orrible to you?" she whispered to Jack during a lull in a game of *Blind Man's Bluff.*

Amy made Ronnie the centre of all her attention. She praised everything that he did and listened to all he said with a look of artificial reverenceon her pretty face. She was immune to Bill's pointed comments about her performance and it was only after her mother had taken her aside for a few quiet words did her manner return to something like normal. Even so she did not resume her normal demeanour towards Jack. Since their time at infant school she had always placed him on a pedestal and would have no bad word said against him. In recent years, when they had reached an age when boys and girls became conscious of their sexuality, Jack had begun to find her attention a little irritating and at times embarrassing. To him, she was just another friend, almost a sister. So when he and Lil took their leave, her parting words, which she had meant to hurt and make him jealous, came somewhat as a form of liberation.

They had said goodbye to all those in the parlour and Jack had made arrangements to meet Bill and Ronnie on Boxing Day. Amy escorted them to the door. She kissed Lil goodnight and then fixed Jack with her green eyes, and gave him a look of profound seriousness.

"I shan't be writing to you again, Jack," she delivered the words like a court sentence.

"Oh!" was his disappointing reply, "that's okay, it's gonna be tough this term and you will soon be starting work so we're both gonna be busy," he gave her a smile full of innocence.

"No, no," she called after them as they stepped out into the frosty night, "I mean that I shall be writing to Ronnie."

He turned, still smiling, "Good, poor ol' Ron ain't got anyone to write to him, he'll appreciate that," he paused."That's kind of you Amy."

The door shut with more force than was really necessary and the two headed home.

"I don't think you were supposed to be pleased Jack," Lil said with wisdom beyond her seven years.

He grinned down at her, "I know, Lil," he released her hand, "come on, I'll race you home."

Chapter Eight

They felt and behaved like 'old salts' when they returned to Keyham on New Year's Eve, they were no longer the new boys. They offered a mixture of advice and scorn to the new drafts of nervous and worried civilians who were embarking on their new and strange life. But in turn they were also treated with a degree of contempt and ridicule by intakes ahead of them.

"It ain't half funny without Jimmy 'ere to boss us about,"Ronnie observed as he laid claim to his old hammock space.

"Yeah," Bill dropped his case on his sailor's box, "he's a proper sailor now, on a ship of the line."

"And he'll be getting 'omeat weekends if he's lucky," Jack added.

"That's if his ship stays in Birkenhead," Bill pointed out.

"It will," Jack replied knowledgeably, "he told me that she'll do a couple of week's sea trails before she joins the fleet and she ain't even been commissioned yet."

"Hey!"Ronnie changed the subject, "what if that gorilla Hindle comes looking for us?"

The three of them exchanged worried looks and began unpacking their small cases into their boxes. Jack, lovingly put Romin's gift to him, a leather bound copy of Kipling's *Soldiers Three*, under his clean PT kit and placed his best tunic on top of it as protection

"It won't be us he's after," Jack said unconvincingly, "it was Jimmy that smacked 'im."

"Yeah, but he's gone but we're still 'ere and we could easily bump into 'im,"Ronnie went to window and looked out as though the possibility was imminent.

"Right you maggots!" the voice boomed through the mess diverting their worries. A very physical looking PTI loomed in the open door, "outside in PT kit in five minutes," he grinned maliciously, "let's run off some of that Christmas pud you've been ramming down your 'orrible little necks over the past week."

Training had been demanding and physically hard up to this point but now it took a new turn. The physical aspect was retained in the form of two periods of PT a week and one sports afternoon, the square bashing reduced noticeably and small arms training ceased. Now they were being trained for their trades. As far as the navy was concerned they were competent sailors, to a point.The knowledge that they had acquired thus far would be tempered and widened by experience aboard ship, and the majority of lessons now took place in classrooms.In the three friend's cases, hands on training with 6-inch guns; they were all destined to be Sight-Setters.

The class work was arduous for those how did not have a natural bent for mathematics. So much had to be learnt; wind deflection, elevation and calculating the mean point of impact of the fall of shot. Although the GO, Gunnery Officer, would normally do these calculations when in battle, it was imperative that all of the gun crew had some ability, as everyman in the team had to learn the job of all the other members. The nine men in a gun team had a lot to learn. Each individual, of course, was most skilled in his own task but in the case of a member of the team becoming wounded or killed his position could be filled and the gun would still be able to function.

Jack enjoyed this phase of their training. Although he was not outstandingly good at maths he surprised himself how easily he mastered the calculations needed in gunnery. Most of all he enjoyed the hands on training on the 6-inch QF gun, the type they were most likely to be using when they joined their ships. It was used as secondary armament on the mighty Dreadnoughts and as the main defence on cruisers and, the faster, light cruisers.

Nine fresh faced and eager youths stood at post behind the grey gun that thrust its ten feet long barrel out, menacingly, over the River Dart. Before them stood Petty Officer Bell, a small man with a weathered face that resembled a walnut and eyes, black as coal that squinted as if he was permanently looking into a tropical sun.

'Ding Dong', as he was known, patted the guns armour shield almost lovingly, "This 'ere, is the Quick Firing 6-inch naval gun, one of the finest pieces of 'ardware on any of His Majesty's Ships." He shook his head as if surprised by his own words, "Oh, there's bigger pieces alright, the Dreadnoughts carry mighty 10 and 15-inchers," he narrowed his eyes, "but they is slow, one round a minute," he patted the gun again, "but this little beauty can deliver five, one hundred pound shells every minute, and seven with a good crew manning 'er." He paused while they absorbed this information, and then went on."She can traverse 150 degrees, plus and minus and she can depress minus five and elevate plus 20 degrees. No other naval gun can match this versatility. Yes, Asher."

"Why can it fire so much faster than other guns, Sir?"

"I'm glad you asked me that young fellah, but I would 'ave come to it during the course of this lesson," he walked to the rear of the gun where a shell and cartridge stood and picked up the former. "This 'ere is the shell, the bit that does all the damage, it weighs one hundred pounds and it is pushed along by this chap, the cartridge," he tapped a large brass case, "which contains the propellant. Now all the larger calibre guns is breechloaders and behind the shell there is a cloth bag full of propellant and then a percussion tube. It all takes time, whereas this little beauty, if little is the right description, is bunged in the breech with the cartridge right behind an Bob's yerflippin uncle,"he moved further to the rear of the gun, "Right, take station."

They all moved the positions that had been allocated at the start of the lesson; Bill was at the elevating wheel in the role of gun layer and Jack was on the right and in line with the breech as breech worker. The gun training began and they put the theory they had learned thus far intosweaty practice. For an hour and a half they rehearsed the many drills from clearing for action to securing the gun at end of firing. After a ten-minute break, they started again but this time in different roles, each one physically arduous and mentally demanding. For a gun team to operate efficiently their concentration had to be total. The slightest lapse by a single member was enough to throw the whole team into a state of instability that brought down the wrath of PO Bell on their collective heads.

"Concentrate, concentrate," he screamed skipping round the gun pushing and pulling theslow-witted and idle, "the shells is raining down on yer, yer all gonna die."

By the end of a fortnight they were slick, quick and confident and though they may have appeared impressive to the uninitiated, PO Bell still spotted minor mistakes that he considered would adversely affect the smooth efficiency of the team.

"Cornwell, you lazy little bleeder, step back sharper after closing the breech, split seconds count, they're the difference between life an' death."

Ronnie, in the role of Sight-Setter, stumbled over the wordsas he relayed the GO's orders to the team.

"He's speaking the King's, bleeding, English, Raven," he stopped hopping in front of Ronnie his puce face inches away, "he's telling you the words to say, what's your bleeding problem with that?"

Like most instructors at Keyham, the students realised that George Bell's bark was far worse than his bite and his enthusiasm for his calling was infectious, the finest quality in a teacher. Another characteristicthat he shared with other staff was that he was nearing the end of his service and this did not please him. He loved the 'Andrew' and found it difficult to contemplate life as a civilian. The war was, horrific though it may be, putting off that awful day as experienced instructors were desperately needed.

As intimated, he was a kindly and, reasonably patientman and providing his pupils were applying themselves with the diligence that he thought the subject of gunnery deserved, he could be forgiving as well as tolerant, but when Ronnie bungled another sighting orderthe little PO lost control.

"Get off my bleeding gun, you useless article," he screamed, approaching the fearful Ronnie like a ferret after a rabbit. "See that," he pointed at the steep slope that extended down to the barrack boundary at the Saltash Road.

"Sir,"Ronniereplied, his eyes wide and as full of dread as any rabbit cornered by a ferret.

"Right, well take your lazy bones down there at the double an' be back 'ere in less than five minutes or you'll do it again. Move!"

Ronnie took off at a run knowing the task was beyond any human.Thefour hundred yard run to the fence was easy enough but the return,up the steep grassy bank, was another matter.He did the run three times before PO Bell considered that he had been sufficiently punished.Ronnie stood, red faced and sweating, at the rear of the gun trying to ignore the smirks and winks of his messmates, as he waited for the PO's attention and release from his chastisement.

"Perhaps that'll concentrate yer mind Raven,"he said when he had finished readjusting the guns sights after the last problem, "an' you lot can wipe those smiles of yer faces," he added without turning to look at them, "I'll lay odds you'll all get a taste o' that little 'ill afore yer leave Keyham."

As the days passed, Ding Dong's words were proved only too true and nobody escaped the dreaded hill run, and nobody thought that they had deserved it.

"I'm sure 'e only does it for a laugh," Bill complained after his third sentence.

But under the diminutive cockney's beady eye and mixture of encouragement, expertise and threat of the lung-bursting hill, they were gradually forged from clumsy, ignorant youths into a slick team, well versed with the gun they attended and their individual roles in its effectiveness as a deadly weapon of war.

The days passed quickly, nobody had the chance to become bored. The hours were filled with lessons and the evenings with cleaning, for which the navy is celebrated, and attention to their kit and uniforms. And just to make sure that they were fully occupied it was necessary to brush up on the days lessons.

They had little money to spend, six shillings (30pence) a week did not usually extend far beyond purchasing the required cleaning materials. Postal orders from their families and food parcels were great occasions as were visits to the canteen on receipt of a postal order. Homesickness was a thing of the past but letters were always looked forward too by all servicemen.

"I've got five bob," Bill beamed at Jack.

They had just had post call and those lucky enough to get letters sat around the mess updating themselves with the happenings at home.Normally such an announcement would have interested Jack greatly as they always shared what they received; taking Ronnie into their bond, for as an orphan he never received parcels or postal orders, but now he was at least getting letters as Amy had promised.

The letter that gripped Jack's attention was from Romin, he recognised her handwriting and the expensive envelope, and he had not had a letter for over two weeks. He carefully slit the envelope with his jack knife taking care to make a clean cut. He unfolded the two sheets and began to read, the blood drained from his face as he read;

*"Dearest Jack,"*she wrote, *"I am sorry that I have not answered your, very welcome, letters over the past weeks and I have struggled to apply myself even now. On the 8ᵗʰ of March we heard the terrible news that my beloved brother had succumbed to his wounds and died. Needless to say I was, and still am, devastated.*

My parents wanted to bring his body home for burial in our family vault but his last request was that he lay, for eternity, with those of his regiment who had already died and although I would have liked a place to have visited him on a regular basis I am glad that he now lies with the comrades whom he so admired and loved.

Please forgive me for such a brief letter bearing only news of my anguish, but in a few weeks I will be recovered sufficiently to write in a more positive mien.

I hope you will continue to write, as I find your letters so uplifting.

Your friend always, Romin."

"What's up, mon?"Ronnie sat down beside him at the mess table;"you look shattered," a look of genuine concern had spread across Ronnie's narrow face.

Jack looked sideways at him, stunned. He handed him the letter, "Read that," he covered his face with his hands to hide his grief from the rest of the mess. They would soon be at war themselves; tears were out of the question.

He had only met Clive on three occasions and he was from a class that would not normally have given his likes the time of day, but his hospitality and attention to Jack had been completely sincere. Despite the great social gap Jack had felt more than comfortable in their exchanges. He uncovered his face, "He was a really nice fellah, Ron,as me mum would say, he had no edge on 'im."

Ronnie handed back the letter looking even more morose, "I suppose I'm lucky in a way," he placed a comforting arm round Jacks shoulder.

"How's that?"

"I ain't got anyone to lose, 'ave I?"

"What about us, yer mates?"

"Oh yeah, but we ain't gonna get killed are we mon," he cheered a little, "we're gonna get to be old jack tars an' come back 'ere as instructors an' make life hell for the nozzers," he got to his feet, "Come on, Asher's gone to the canteen, he said he'd buy us a bun an' a ginger beer."

As they arrived at the canteen door Bill hurtled out flushed and a look of consternation on his freckled face.

"What's up?"Ronnie asked.

"He's is in there," he gasped as they caught up with him.

"Who?" Jackgrabbed his arm but was unable to halt his friend's flight.

"The bloke that Jimmy bashed, what's his name...? Hindle."

"Did he recognise yer?"Ronnie asked as he caught up.

"I dunno, I didn't 'ang around to find out."

*

Chief Fitzgerald growled the crowded hall to attention as Captain Chapman strode down the aisle and took up position on the low stage.He was of short andsquare stature sporting a black beard that was becoming salted with grey. Intelligent grey eyes swept the hall with a steeliness that had struck fear into the heart many a ratingthat had transgressed and found himself on Captains interview.

"Stand them easy, Chief," he placed his cap on the lectern in front of him and surveyed the young faces. He felt a shadow of guilt enfold him as he looked around the gathering; he had prepared them for war, a war in which many of them would die or be maimed for the rest of their lives. And those who would be maimed would be forgotten and neglected as fighting men had always been ever since the first day that nation's had sent their young men to die for the rich and powerful. He was too old, his fighting days were over.

Two days earlier Oswald Chapman had attended a lecture given by his brother, Gareth, who was a lecturer in history at Oxford. Gareth had given the lecture from his wheelchair having become a double amputee whilst serving as a company commander with the Rifle Brigade at the relief of Ladysmith, during the Boer War. His position, education and modest wealth had saved him from the deprivation and suffering that had to be borne by old soldiers less fortunate.But he was a champion of their cause and did everything that he could, through his regiments association, to help those in need.

The opening words of Gareth's lecture sprang to Captain Chapman's mind as he gazed in brief silence at the youthful audience before him.He had said; *studying history will move you to love the soldier, hate the businessman and despise the politician.* Oswald knew that the word soldier could be justifiably replaced with, sailor.

He cleared his throat, "It is normal practice for me to give a talk in your last week of training but sadly I will not be here so to do, and therefore you will have to suffer this ordeal a little earlier than is customary. Well done to you all for coming this far. The transition from civilian to sailor is not an easy change to make and you should all be proud of what you have achieved, and you should be even more fulfilled at the thought of the great family that you are about to join."He paused and leaned forward on the lectern, "I am sure that throughout your training you have been constantly reminded that you are joining the finest navy in the world and no honest sailor from other navies would deny that claim.As a Sight-Setter, your role is vital in the operation of the ships armoury, as is the role of all the other members of the guns crew, but unless you are steady and alert the gun will be ineffective if the target is missed. The lives of your shipmates will depend on your coolness and steadfastness in the face of great danger.

"I do not intend to alarm you, but it is one thing to relay the GO's orders in the calm environment of a training lesson, but it is quite another thing in the mind-numbing roar of a naval engagement, with shells crashing around you and the deafening din of your own gun". He turned to a young gunnery officer who had accompanied him into the hall, "Have they experienced live firing yet, Anthony?"

"Next week, Sir."

The Captain's brows knitted to convey the seriousness of what he was about to say."You will be frightened when you first go into battle, boys, everybody is. It is natural and if anyone tells you that he isn't afraid, then he is either a liar or a fool and you'd be best advised to avoid both. Without fear there is no courage, for courage is merely the conquering of fear." Another pause followed, Captain Chapman was not performing, and his speech came from the heart. "Remember your duty; your duty to your country, to your King and most importantly your duty to your shipmates. If you do your duty no man can fault you, always remember that. You can make mistakes and you will be admonished but forgiven, but fail to do your duty and you will have failed as a member of this great family." His mood lightened."Good luck to you all and may God go with you."

As the Captain picked up his cap and turned from the lectern the CPO brought them to attention.

*

In his head phones Bill heard the GO's order and he repeated it with a pounding heart.

"Fire!"

They were all unprepared for the noise. They had heard firing out at sea and had imagined what it would sound like when in close proximity to a gun, but even so they were numbed and disorientated by the hard, flat, metallic crash, of the six-pounder. Bill was conscious of a distant voice followed by a louder one close at hand and then something hard jabbing him in the ribs.

"Pass the bluidy order you idiot," the marine sergeant was almost apoplectic.

Bill gathered his wits in time to hear the GO repeating the order."Range, four thousand," he echoed, "deflection ten knots...bearing, three, two, five degrees."

Bodies moved like clockwork; hands spun wheels and pulled levers and the great barrel turned and rose to engage the target.

They were on board an ancient cruiser ten miles off Plymouth, in the mouth of the English Channel, having their first taste of live firing under the jaundiced eye of a sergeant from the Royal Marine Artillery. Wallace Cassanach was infamous for his short temper even when things were going well, and this was not such a day.

He grabbed the communication mouthpiece, "Permission to suspend firing, Sir," a garbled reply along the pipe sufficed.

Cassanach bore down on Bill like an eagle falling on its prey, "You are a useless little, cretin," he bellowed, inches from Bill's face, "what are you?"

"A useless little cretin, Sergeant," Bill replied cringing from the NCO's breath which was mixture of last night's beer, tobacco and bad teeth.

"What are you laughing at?" he jabbed a long, talon like finger under Jacks nose.

"Nothin', Sergeant," he struggled to keep a straight face.

"Give 'im the headset," he snapped at Bill, "let's see if he can do any better," he blew into the comms tube, "Ready to continue firing, Sir."

Adrenaline rushed through Jack's veins as he made the final adjustment to the leather helmet that contained the earpieces, through which the GO's orders would come. His nostrils were filled with stench of cordite, hot metal and the bracing sea air. He experienced a sense of power the like of which he had never felt before. His single word would provoke this mighty weapon to life, hurling a hundred pounds of devastation, thousands of yards across the rolling grey sea, at an old hulk awaiting its end.

He delivered the GO's instruction in a clear loud voice, hoping that the rest of the gun crew did not detect the tremor of excitement in his words and mistake it for fear.

Then the order came, "Fire!" he bawled.

Despite having already experienced one mighty detonation, they were no less shocked by the second. By the time that they had discharged the twenty rounds allocated for this training session, they were all becoming more comfortable with the impact of each discharge but the ringing in their ears caused the conversations, on the way back to land, to be held in raised voices.

Chapter Nine

The day had finally arrived; their term of training was at an end. Hardy Mess paraded outside of the Training Office in their best uniforms with all of their worldly goods stuffed into their kitbags that lay on the floor in front of them. The spring sunshine warmed their backs and a cool westerly breeze ruffled the large collars of their uniforms. The excitement that they all felt was tarnished by the sadness of the many goodbyes that were to be suffered as they disbursed throughout the navy, possibly, never to meet again. Few considered the possibility that they may be killed during the coming months; they possessedthe immortality that accompanies youth.

The pursers clerk emerged from the office carrying a millboard on which was clipped a sheet of paper. He was a man of slight build and neat appearance but he was accompanied by an enormous rating whose uniform was anything but natty.

Jack nudged Bill, "Look who it is," he hissed anxiously, "its..."

"I can bloody see," Bill replied through gritted teeth.

"Hey,"Ronnie joined in, "it's that fellah, Hindle."

"We know," they whispered in unison.

The clerk cut short any further discussion, "Now listen in," the murmuring and fidgeting stopped, "I will first call out the name of a ship and then all those named after that will come forward and receive their joining orders from my mate here," he indicated

Maurice. "As well as your joining orders, you will get a travel warrant home, a week's leave passand the warrant to join your ship, clear?" Nods and more muttering of affirmation answered the question."Do not lose any of these documents, if you do and fail to join your ship on time, you will be posted as absent. Right," the clerk continued, "when I call out the ship I will also tell you the port of joining," he cleared his throat. "HMS *Indefatigable*, Newcastle," he went on to name those joining the ill-fated Dreadnought.

Within ten minutes the three friends were left on their own all other mess members had received their ships and documents and were heading for the main gate and a week's welcome leave.

"Asher, Raven and Cornwell?" the clerk asked, they nodded, "right, HMS *Chester* at Birkenhead."

Jack took his documents from Hindle with a beating heart. There was a slight, glimmer of recognition in the bully's piggy eyes but it was something that his brain could not register in the brief meeting and the three of them hurried away hoping that Hindle was not going on leave that day.

*

It was the first day of May, sun was bright and their hearts light as they strolled along Brompton Road wallowing in the goodwill and friendly greetings of old acquaintances and friends. In 1915, young men in uniform were treated with respect and hailed as heroes; a mere four years later would see the same young men, now civilians and many maimed, shunned and abused by an ungrateful populous. The least grateful being those who had avoided the field of battle, staying behind to make many small and large fortunes from the sacrifice of others.

But the three boys were not aware of this, though history proved the point, and they soaked up the warmth and generosity. Old men in pub doorways tried to ply them with drink.

"Thanks, but we ain't allowed to take strong drink,"Ronnie explained to two old men sat on a bench outside The Pig and Firkin.

"Not allowed a drink?" the fat one said with genuine horror, 'd'you 'ear that Bert, a matelot who don't drink."

"That's new one on me 'Arry," Bert replied wiping the froth from his moustache with the back of his hand, "a blooming Jack Tar refusing a tipple – unheard of," he took another pull at his pint and grinned at the boys. "They only looks like nippers t' me 'Arry."

"Go on then, mon,"Ronnie grinned, "I'll accept yer generous offer, mine's a pale ale."

"An' what about you two?"Bert got to his feet.

Bill was adamant, "Naw, thanks anyway," tempted though he was to act the man in a man's world. He hoped that he would be able to summon up the courage to face the Germans but he knew that he would be unable to muster enough nerve to face his mother smelling of beer.After a slight hesitation Jack also refused knowing he was going to visit Romin later in the day.

"You shouldn't really have beer Ronnie," Bill warned, again with his mother in mind but giving another reason, "it's against the rules you know."

"Garn," Harry scoffed, "rules is for the guidance of wise men and the obedience of fools. Get the boy 'is beer Bert and bring his two mates a couple of ginger beers."

They sat with the old men for a while and listened to their tales of past wars. Both had served across the globe, from India to the Sudan, and had bloodcurdling, funny and sad stories to relate about their adventures.Most of them embellished to make the story all the better.

"Yeah, we've both seen a bit of fighting," Bert said seriously as they prepared to part, "but I'll tell yer this boys, what we went through don't compare wiv what's going on over there," he nodded in the direction that he considered France lay, "this country has never taken such casualties."

"That's a fact," Harry added, "but the sacrifice you fellahs are making will be forgotten weeks after it's all over, you mark my words."

It was difficult to believe the old soldiers prophecy as they continued their way through the Saturday morning shoppers. Greetings and wishes of goodwill fell upon them like warm rain in a summer storm. Looks of envy from youths, too young to enlist, were only bettered by coy glances of admiration from young girls. As they passed a queue of people outside the swimming baths, they were slightly embarrassed, but secretly pleased, when those gathered began to applaud and two small girls asked for their autographs.They parted at the tram terminal, Ronnie and Bill had planned a trip along the Thames on a river taxi and Jack was going to visit Sikkim Hall.

"Don't be making any plans to meet her ladyship on Friday," Bill said as they went their separate ways, "the fair's on in Little Ilford Park, it'll be fun."

"Ere, Jackie boy,"Ronnie called after him loudly, the pint of beer was having some effect, "see if yer can find me an' Bill a duchess too," he laughed loudly at his own joke.

*

Megan met him as he rounded the side of the hall and the despondency of the household was apparent in her face.

"Hello Jack," she hugged him and gave him an unconvincing smile.

"Hello Megan, sad isn't it," then a terrible thought came to him, "Nobby's all right ain't he?"

"Yes love, he's hoping to get home for a spot of leave soon," she led him by the arm through the kitchen garden speaking softly as they went. "Sir James has given his permission for Miss Romin to meet you; she's painting in the summer house. She has taken Clive's death very badly; they were very close you know."

"Yeah, I know."

"Some days she wants to talk about him and others she won't mention him, so let her be the first to raise the subject otherwise, well, she'll be in tears till bedtime," she stopped at the gate that led out into the rose garden. "She never mentions his death, all she talks about, when she does talk about him, are the happy times she had with him in her childhood,"she gave him a reassuring smile and patted his arm, "she is so looking forward to seeing you," she wagged an intimidating finger at him, "Don't you dare go and get yourself killed, Jack Cornwell, that would be the end of her."

"Garn, Megan," he joked, "Fritz won't get me."

"I certainly hope not, Jack," she led him along a path that dissected the beds of rose bushes, "Go to the end of this path and turn left, you'll see the summer house by the pond."

The open side of the house was towards him and Romin sat on a cane chair engrossed in what she was doing. She had a large drawing pad on her knee and was intent on her work. Puck, who was curled up at her feet, spotted him and began to bark.

Romin looked up and smiled, "Jack," she got to her feet and ran to meet him. Taking his hand she led him back to the summerhouse, "It is so good to see you. Tell me how you are. I know you write regularly but it's not the same as talking," she poured him a glass of orange and handed it to him."You say you're to join a ship called *Chester*..," she stopped mid-sentence, a look of concern on her face, "I haven't let you say a word," she shook her head, "half the time I have no idea what I'm gabbling on about, I just talk for the sake of it."Her

101

concerned expression became one of anguish, "It's Clive," she sank limply into the chair beside him and took his hand.

Jack leaned forward, "It must have been 'orrible."

"It still is, I can't begin to explain the pain of it all and I haven't felt able to explain this deep hurt to others," she paused and she seemed to relax, "But now you're here and I know I have a soul mate."Jack nodded unsure of what to say. "You will have to take his place as my big brother Jack."Once more he was lost for words and nodded again."It was bad enough hearing that John was missing and Clive wounded, little did I know just how bad things were to get."

"Still no word about John?"

"Sadly no, poor Mister Kipling is going to have to face the awful truth eventually," the sadness was suddenly replaced by anger. "It's such an awful waste of good men with so much to offer the world," the anger became poignancy."Promise me Jack that you will come through this bedlam safe, no heroics."

"It's a bit different on a ship, it's not like being in the army where you dash off an' win a medal. In the navy you just have to go where the ship goes, don't suppose there'll be much chance to win medals."

Her spirits appeared to lift, "Enough of this maudlin talk, we have to keep faith, hope for the best and pray," she paused,"I pray for you every night, Jack."

He was moved, "That's nice, thanks."

She grimaced, "For what good it'll do you; I also prayed for Clive."

They talked until the warmth left the air and dusk began to descend over the garden. Jack felt at ease. It was peaceful in the large garden and the evening was scented by the climbing roses that clambered over the summerhouse walls.

"Me and Bill and Ron are going to the fair on Little Ilford Park on Friday," he said, unplanned, "d'you think you'd be able to come as well?"

Her enthusiasm was real, "Oh, that would be wonderful, it would be just what I need," a look of determination tempered her eagerness, "I will have to indulge in a little subterfuge though. I know that if I seek permission it will be unlikely to be forthcoming," her mood brightened, "but I am sure Megan can be recruited to assist in this enterprise."

When Megan came to say that it was time for Jack to leave, she agreed, with a hint of reluctance, to accompany Romin to the fair.

"I'm sure that Master Clive would have approved," she said as they walked back towards the house.

*

The light drizzle that had fallen for most of the day did not dampen the spirits of those who gathered on Little Ilford Park to enjoy the annual fair. The greyness of the evening added to the atmosphere giving the lights of the booths and merry-go-rounds a more exciting and mystical aura.A barrel organ competed loudly with the cries of the fairground barkers seeking to attract the attention of the public as they picked their way carefully over the ground that became muddier by the minute.

"I wish I hadn't put me best boots on," Bill moaned as he inspected the glutinous mud that despoiled his once gleaming footwear.

"They'll clean easy enough,"Ronnie reassured him, "it's not like they're scuffed, that would be a pain."

"Honestly!" Amy scoffed, "What a fuss over a little mud."

They waited by the main entrance to the park, Jack was subdued, Romin had not yet arrived. They

103

others were becoming impatient and it was Amy who was most vocal in their frustration.

"It's well past the time you arranged Jack, it really is inconsiderate,"

"Shut up Amy, they've got a long way to come." Bill rebuked.

"Listen, you all go in," Jack was feeling a little uncomfortable. He had expected Amy to be difficult and he thought he would be able handle the situation but the waiting was likely to compound the problem, "we'll find you easy enough."

This was agreed.

"If she bothers turning up at all," was Amy's parting shot, "the upper classes don't like mixing with the likes of us."

"Don't Amy like you anymore Jack?" Lil asked when the others had left.

"She don't like me being friends with Romin," he explained.

"I'm looking forward to meeting your new girlfriend," Lil grinned up at him.

"She ain't really my girlfriend, Lil," he craned to see over the milling throng, "she's a friend; rich girls don't 'ave boyfriends from poor families."

"Oh, but she's nice to you?"

He gave her hug, "Yeah, she's very nice," he waved, "here she is."

Romin and Megan emerged from the multitude beneath shining umbrellas, smiling and a little breathless.

"Sorry we're late Jack," Megan apologised, "it took longer than we thought."

"It's only a few minutes, I'm just glad you found it alright. This is my little sister, Lil. It's Lily really but me mum's called Lily, so it's Lil."

Lil was always shy when she met people for the first time as is the case with most small children, but Romin's easy manner quickly overcame the awkwardness, she took Lil by the hand and led them all into the throng.

"I'm so excited," she beamed, "I can't remember when I last rode on a tram or bus, and now this," she waved at the masses swarming over the rides and booths. She bent down to Lil, "Shall we go on that large helter-skelter?" Lil nodded, smiling, "come on then."

They caught up with the others at the coconut shy where Ronnie and Bill were engaged in a spirited contest the end of which saw the latter triumphant with three nuts dislodged.But all that he had as proof of his marksmanship was small vase, which he later broke whilst operating a swing boat.

Despite Jacks warnings, and his own promise to himself, Bill reverted to a forelock-tugging peasant in Romin's presence. Whether it was her beauty or her status that overwhelmed him, even he was not certain, but the fact that he was in awe of her was without doubt. His mother would have been delighted with this young girl's effect on her son, he was almost dumbstruck, and on the occasions that he could muster speech he became tongue tied and pathetically obsequious.In contrast, Amy became surly and devoid of her natural Christianity. She forced herself to portray aveneer of civility but it was painfully transparent, and whereas Mrs Asher would have been pleased with her son's manner she would have been appalled by her daughters.Jack spent most of the evening shielding Romin from the conflicting conduct of his friends by directing them to differing entertainments.

"Here,Ronnie, why don't you try and win Amy one of those dolls,"he suggested as they paused in front of a shooting gallery.

Megan assisted, "Go on Ronnie," she urged, "in fact why don't we all compete, I've used my brother's guns back at home, so I'm open to all challengers," she turned to the man running the gallery, "how much?"

"A penny for ten shots my lovely," he pushed a small tin, containing the pellets, towards her.

"Come on then lass,"Ronnie slapped his penny on the counter, "never let it be said that a Geordie ducked a dare. Right Amy, which of those d'you want?"

"Let's make a contest of it," Bill joined in finding his voice and producing a coin, "us all being Sight-Setters. Are you game, Jack?"

But Jack was already guiding Romin away from the group, "Romin wants a go on the hobby horses," he called over his shoulder.

"Do I?"

"Shhh!" he took her into the crowd, "Let's get away for a while, Amy's being a grump and Bill...well Bill's gone loopy, the way he is with you..."

She grinned impishly, "I think he's very charming."

"Very barmy more like."

"Can I stay and watch." Lil asked.

"Go on then,"he agreed, "but don't wander off."

Romin dragged him to a halt in front of a gaudy tent with a sign proclaiming the presence of a fortuneteller.

"Shall we?"

"You don't believe in..."

"It could be amusing," she encouraged, "come on let's try."

"Come in, dearie," a disembodied voice called from inside the tent, "know the future and be prepared."

Cautiously they entered through the heavy curtains that covered the entrance. The voice that summoned them was a rich contralto and the small lady sat at the table seemed an unlikely possessor of such commanding timbre. Silver wisps of hair escaped the scarf that covered her head and her face was brown and extremely wrinkled, but her expression was sereneand gentle. On the table stood the inevitable crystal ball reflecting the candles that provided the only illumination in the tent.

She indicated them to sit with an ephemeral wave of her hand, "Ah, a sailor boy. I normally charge a tanner each, but in your case I'll do you both for a tanner." She had a strange accent that Jack thought was faked. He handed her two three-penny bits, which she examined briefly, "I prefer my palm to be crossed with silver."

Before Jack could extract the desired coinage from his pocket Romin passed the lady a sixpenny piece and she handed the two three-pence pieces back to Jack.

She took Romin's hand, "Ladies first," for what seemed a long time she studied Romin's slender hand, Jack suspected this to be part of the act but her opening words caused him to reassess his first impression. "You have recently suffered some dreadful grief, my dear," Romin made no response, either verbal or physical, "someone very close, a relative," still, Romin kept her silence, "a handsome man, a young man."

Jack considered all that she had mentioned so far was pretty safe guesswork. Most families in the country had, so far, lost a loved one and most would have been young. His scepticism returned.

The woman looked into the crystal ball, "He was from the Emerald Isle," this time Romin shook her head, "but I see a shamrock," she insisted, "but it is not green, it is gold." Jack felt his doubts fading again and he heard Romin softly catch her breath. The fortune-teller continued, "you do not want for things of this world little one, but always remember that wealth does not always bring happiness or peace of mind." She leant forward towards Jack with outstretched hand,

"Give me your hand," he found the time that she spent inspecting his palm unnerving, at length she said, "You will have great fame young man, great fame." She drew a hand across her face. "I feel tired," she beckoned Romin closer; she clasped her hand tightly, "I would have preferred to have given you better news, my pretty one."

Outside they paused to gather their composure. Romin looked alarmed and close to tears."She was talking about Clive."

Jack nodded, "It could 'ave been anyone, lots of people 'ave lost family and friends."

"No," she was adamant, "the shamrock."

"Well, there's lots of Irish..."

"The badge of the Irish Guards, have you seen it?"

"What of it?"

"In the centre, there is a golden shamrock,"she sighed deeply and forced a smile."At least you had some good news; you're going to be famous."

Chapter Ten

Extract from ships log 2nd of May 1916 as entered by Captain Robert Neale Lawson: HMS Chester launched by Lady Sandhurst at Cammell Laird shipyard, Birkenhead.

The day arrived for them to leave home and to join their first ship, HMS *Chester*. Jack was glad that he was posted with friends for the excitement was now shaded with a large measure of apprehension that came close to being fear. His family did not accompany him to the station as they did when he enlisted, that had been the greatest wrench for them all.

Lily had become accustomed to her son being parted from her but this parting had regurgitated all of the numbing fear that she had experienced when he had left for the first time. She knew now that her initial misgivings had been groundless but now her child was going off to engage in war, the most violent war that the world had ever experienced. She had seen so many telegram boys en-route to unsuspecting homes bearing their dreadful tidings and her heart had gone out to the unknown mother or wife. But now she knew that if she saw one of those blue clad youths on a red bike enter her street then she would probably die of a heart attack before he raised the knocker. With a husband and son in the army, and now Jack off to join his ship, the odds were very high that.... She could not have that concluding thought.

They had hugged at the door with Bill and Ronnie close by, waiting. Lil had been tearful but not as hysterical as the first parting. There was a look of resignation on her young face as she looked up at the brother that she so loved.

"Come back to me, Jack," she said softly, hugging his waist.

"Course I will, daft kid."

Lily could see his eyes filling and knew that he would not want to be seen crying in front of his ship mates so she felt that she must conceal her emotion.

"They're all off on a lovely cruise, aren't you boys?" she said as cheerily as she could as Jack exchanged a manly handshake with his younger brother,George.

They stood at the door watching the three young sailors, jauntily heading off down the street, kit bags on their shoulders and caps at rakish angles. Lily closed the door and sank to the floor, her body wracked with sobs.

The train to Liverpool was packed with sailors and in this familiar atmosphere Jack's misgivings quickly evaporated. The banter and yarns of their travelling companions, many of them with years of service behind them, kept them entertained and laughing throughout the journey.

Outside Lime Street Station rows of buses and trucks waited to take the horde of blue jackets to their ships that were tied up at various points on the Mersey. Petty officers, three stripers and Royal Marine NCOs directed the seething mariners to the correct transport. Most of them held crudely fashioned cards stating the names of ships."

"Look,"Ronnie pointed excitedly, "that says *Birkenhead* and *Chester*."

A hoaryand grey-bearded three striper held the card aloft and walked slowly to and fro in front of the station with a nonchalant air.

"Are you for HMS *Chester*, mate?"

The old sailor stopped and eyed Bill calmly, "An' what gives you the idea that I be your mate, sparky?"

Bill hesitated, "Well, I was just trying to be friendly," he said.

The old sailor's nut-brown face was momentarily impassive but then slowly split in a twisted grin.

"Well shipmate, that's alright then," he winked, "an' if you was to cast a weather eye over my cap tally you'd 'ave the answer to your question and that's confirmed by this 'ere card I'm 'olding in my 'and." His cap tally bore words HMS *Chester*.

*

Ships log 4th of May 1916. Received eleven ratings from Chatham and three Boys from Keyham.

The two newly commissioned light cruisers lay stern to stern alongside the North Jetty of Birkenhead Dock. The quay, and the decks of both ships,swarmedwith activity. Long necked cranes dangled over the ships decks like inquisitive herons, and human chains of blue clad men, hand balled crates and sacks from the quay, across the decks and into the holds. At the bow of HMS *Birkenhead* a score of men attacked a huge pile of coal with shovels, filling buckets that were then swung onto the deck by rope and pulley. All of those involved were as black as the coal that they were handling.

They negotiated the gangway with difficulty, hampered by their kit and the sweating working party. Following the example of the rating leading them, they paused at the head of the gangway, faced the quarterdeck and saluted in the tradition of the Royal Navy since the day that Lord Nelson fell, mortally wounded at that place.

"Sing out your names," an AB instructed as he waited their arrival, clipboard in hand. "Raven an' Asher Red Watch, foller 'im," he indicated a rating who led them below. "Cornwell, White Watch, foller 'im."

A heavily built rating stepped forward and punched Jack on the upper arm, "Jackie!"

111

"Jimmy!" Jack was overjoyed; his heart had sunk when the other two had been separated from him but now he had found an old friend and felt all the better for it. "I thought you'd gone to *Birkenhead*, Jimmy."

"I had," Jimmy replied as he led the way down a ladder into the bowels of the ship, "but Lord Beatty sent for me an' he sez; Jim lad, we 'ave three nozzers joining *Chester* an' they're little better than useless, so you better get along there to keep yer eye on 'em. Here we are." They had reached a mess with rows of neatly lashed hammocks above lines of sailors' boxes, "This is yer new 'ome Jackie. Stow yer kit and then we'll go up and report to the Writers office."

With Jimmy's help Jack quickly stowed his kit,"You're on the first dog watch with me so we'll have to be first to mess 'cos' were on at four."

"What do we do?" Jack asked a little concerned to find himself on duty so soon after joining.

"Nothing to it," Jimmy assured him, "run messages, get the officer of the watch mugs o' tea and cocoa andbe a general dogsbody. It's only for two hours. Come on we'll meet those other two reprobates at the Writers."

In comparison to other vessels in the Grand Fleet,HMS *Chester*, a light cruiser, was one the smaller ships. Even so, for the three new crew members it was an enormous collection of passages, ladders and messes that all appeared identical, and it would be a number of days before they could go directly to their own mess or gun station without getting lost. *Chester* had a complement of 500hands; her length was 430 feet and she displaced 5,795 tons.

"It'll be better when we get to sea," Jimmy told them, "there's too much graft in port, fatigues and such."

"I tell you, mon,"Ronnie looked worried, "I don't fancy that job those poor buggers were doing, loading all that bloody coal, I only joined up to get away from the mines."

"Not much fear of tha,Ronnie," Jimmy grinned, "*Chester* has been converted to oil. You can see why I was glad when they transferred me."

*

Ships log 5th of May. At sea, 1020 working up main engines and full speed trials, exercised General Quarters.

The sound of the klaxon horn filled the ship with the threat of great danger, and even though the crew knew that it was only a training exercise, they went to their battle stations with all of the urgency of men going into action.

Jack had never experienced such exhilaration; the spray from the bow curled over the gun shield and the fresh North Sea wind tugged at their bell-bottomed trousers. He had worn his grin for so long that his face was aching. HMS*Chester* tore through the waves, on a heading of south by southwest, at 26 knots, her maximum speed. He believed that they were invulnerable surrounded by armour and fairly flying over the choppy sea, how could any enemy gunner possible do them damage.

Hehad been put into the forecastle gun teamas Sight-Setter. He was lucky in that his position in the team was on the left of the gun and close up to the shield, so he was protected from the worst of the spray and wind. The rest of the gun crew extended in two lines away from the gun four on each side,more exposed to the elements and enemy action.

Chester was armed with 10, 5.5-inch guns and although the boys had trained on the 6-inch QF gun, this did not cause them any problems as they were virtually the same weapon,though the 5.5 fired a slightly lighter shell and was easier to handle. But in any case, as Sight-Setters their function went unchanged as it was their task to pass on the orders of the Gunnery Officer as they were received through their headsets.

Ships log 5th of May. 1500 Commenced two-point zig-zag.

The ship reduced speed slightly.

"Stand by for evasive action." The GO's disembodied voice startled him.

"Stand by for evasive action". Jack repeated loudly to the rest of the team not knowing what it meant. He was even more perplexed when the others took hold of various parts of the ironwork.The ship lurched violently as she suddenly altered course, throwing Jack, who was unprepared, against the side shield of the gun and then to his knees. He recovered his position rubbing his damaged parts and suffering the mirth of the rest of the gun crew.

"You'll know what that means next time, lad," Peter Lawless, the breechworker, shouted into the wind. Jack nodded and grinned.

William Smith, the Royal Marine gun layer, leaned across the guns breech, "Be ready for the next tack. We do this to throw off the enemy gunners," he shouted, "makes it harder for themto draw a bead on us."

Jack had only met the rest of the gun crew just before they had left harbour; they seemed a friendly group and all were experienced sailors. The rammer, whom he had already met, was the grey haired AB who had met them at the station and already he had adopted Jack as his responsibility.

"You calls me, Moses," he told Jack as they cleared the breech covers, "names Prophet, but Oi've been stuck with 'Moses' since Oi first enlisted in the Andrew, so Moses it is."

"Why is the Navy called 'The Andrew', Moses?" He asked as they folded the thick canvass covers.

Moses paused, pushed his cap to the back of his grey head, and put on his wise face, "Well, the common story is, and Oi can't vouch for it personally, but back in the days o' Lord Nelson when most of the fleet was made up of forced men, and 'recruited' by the press gang, there was one certain Lieutenant Andrews an' he was so successful when 'e was out looking for 'recruits', as it were, that most who woke up aboard a man-o-war were told they'd been taken by Andrew; so that's how it came to be that you'd joined the Andrew." He stuck a stubby pipe in his mouth, "Roight, come on then lad, let's see if we can get ourselves a wet before they call all hands."

Jack had felt instantly comfortable with the other eight hands that made up the gun crew. Corporal William SmithRoyal Marine Artillery was the Gun-Layer and Commander of the gun. He insisted on being called William or WS,people who shortened his name to Bill were only given one warning, the second reminder was issued physically.Like Moses he was of an indeterminate age but hiswell-worn face, the colour old leather, and his medals told of much service. Jack could detect a touch of kindness in his clear blue eyes, eyes that always seemed half closed and squinting. Jimmy had already warned him that WS was a hard man and was not to be crossed. He never tookerrantsubordinates before the Captain preferring to administer his own justice. When Jack watched him heaving the hundred pound shells, with hands as square and big as shovels, as though they were a mere few pounds, he knew that Jimmy was not exaggerating.

The other six were all a deal older than Jack but accepted him into their number as though he were a seasoned seafarer, but at the same time watched over and guided him from their first meeting. Jack was

115

happy and he was still grinning as HMS *Chester* nosed her way into Birkenhead,just as the early summer sun sank into the North Sea,tingeingwaterthe colour of a blood orange.

Jack's euphoric feeling, though he was not fully aware at the time, was the result of the mystical and incommunicable fact that he belonged to the service. It had always been his dream to join the Navy but like all civilians he did not appreciate the bond that existed among men who shared danger. They had to rely on each other with the total confidence of an absolute commitment of trust,a trust that they would risk their lives to fulfil. They were a family, and though there would be members of the family who they did not particularly like, they would never let them down when their support was called upon.

They met up after they had eaten as Jimmy and Jack were in different messes to Ronnie and Bill. The docks were in darkness and they sat on the deck in front of the forecastle gun, their backs against the shield.

"I tell you Jack, I've never felt so ill in my life, I thought I was gonna die." Bill had been seasick.

"He couldn't man his post,"Ronnie added, "he had t' sit on the deck," he laughed, "yer did look a sorry sight, mon."

"Gawd, I 'ope I'm alright next time."

"You'll be fine," Jimmy said, "I was sick me first time at sea, on Birkenhead, but I'm fine now. Mind," he added ominously, "some are sick every time, Nelson was."

"Garn,"Bill questioned, "he couldn't he have won all those battlesif he'd felt as ill as I did."

"You daft bugger," Jimmy punched him on the shoulder, "they're not sick all the time, it's just every time you set sail, you're alright after a couple of hours."

"I never thought about it," Jack said, "I'd forgotten all about being sea sick."

"I wish I had," Bill shook his head, "I was dreading it."

"That's why you were ill,"Ronnie was confident in his conclusion, "you'd thought about too much."

"Shut up,Ronnie." Bill did not feel the need of his friend's words of wisdom.

*

Ships log 8th of May 0925 Proceed to sea to swing compass. 1040, Commenced gun trials.

When they had trained in gunnery at *Vivid* the noise had shaken them but it was nothing when compared to all ten of HMS *Chester*'s guns being trialled. The guns fired in sequence, so before the blast of the first detonation had passed, the next took place creating a wall of noise that flowed round the ship sucking up the air and engulfing then in the stench of cordite.

Again, Jack was energized by the sheer power that he felt, and once more he experienced a sense of complete security in the power of the ship, its armament and the men around him. This life, the way of the sea, was in the blood of them all, the history books confirmed it. Since Henry the Eighth, Britain hadpossessed the finest navy in the world, a navy that had deterred the countries enemies from even thinking of invasion. And now she was at her mightiest, even the Kaiser's huge building plan had notbrought Germany's Grand Fleet up to the potency of the Royal Navy. But that aside, the Andrew was manned by the finest sailors in the world and no building plan, no matter how grandiose, could rival them.

*

Ships log 13th of May. Hands make and mend clothes. Leave to Red and White watches from 1330 to 1930, boys from 1400 to 1900

"What's Birkenhead like Jimmy,"Ronnie asked as he admired himself in front of the mirror and applied the hairbrush to his dampened hair, "plenty of nice girls"?

"With a gob like yours, you're not even likely to cop of with an ugly one," Jimmy picked up his cap, "come on Raven, it doesn't matter how long you look in the mirror it ain't gonna change the damage that natures done."

Jack gave his collar a quick dusting, "What's the town like though?"

"Nothing to brag about," Jimmy headed for the ladder, "but I must admit I don't remember much about it," he grinned over his shoulder as he mounted the ladder, "I had a little noggin or two."

"I'm up for that,"Ronnie followed him up to the main deck.

"I ain't getting involved with any boozing," Jack said as he followed them.

"Me neither," Bill agreed, "but Ronnie don't care you know, when he stays with us I 'ave to keep me eye on 'im."

They reported to the duty regulator at the head of the gangplank who dutifully noted down their names and time of their departure. He looked up from his list when Jimmy gave his name.

"You get caught drinking today, Cook, and it's the brig for you," he warned, "you've had your chance."

"No worry, chief," Jimmy grinned; a grin that was meant to be reassuring but the regulator saw it as roguish.

"You've been warned, son," he pointed with his pencil and his eyes narrowed, "I'll make sure the shore patrol looks out for you," he jerked his pencil towards the gangplank, "on yer way."

"Did yer get caughtlast time, Jimmy?" Jack asked when they were clear of the ship.

"He was on the patrol that lifted me, but 'is bark is worse than his bite, he let me off with a warning." He led them off towards the town through the shipyard, "Anyway I ain't got enough dosh for drink."

"What are we gonna do then?"Ronnieasked regretfully.

They had reached the dock gate and Jimmy accosted a docker wheeling a trolley, "Hey, mate," the man stopped, "can you tell us how to get to the park."

"The, park?" they all said in unison.

"Shut up you lot," Jimmy turned back to the docker, "this what 'appens when yer bring kids out."

"It's only about fifteen minutes," the man pointed along the road that led out through the gates, "go along here until you see Conway Street on your right, then go along there for about a quarter of a mile and it becomes Park Road, you'll see the park on your left."

"Why are we going to a park?" Jack asked as they headed off as directed.

Jimmy stopped and faced his reluctant shipmates."We haven't got much money, it's a lovely sunny day, it's Saturday and I've been told that the local girls go there looking for sailors, so even with a bloody Geordie and two Cockneys I could still 'ave a good time. Anyway," he added as they continued the journey, "it's got a boating lake so we can get Bill over his seasicknessif we stick 'im out on the lake for a couple of hours."

Bill was not amused by the laughter, "Very funny, it's nice to have the sympathy of yer mess-mates."

When they arrived at the park the two London boys were pleasantly surprised by its size and many features. In fact it was one of the finest parks in the country.It had been designed and built in the early nineteenth century by Sir Joseph Paxton. He had wanted to create the countryside for the town dwellers on Merseyside and he had been so successful in his purpose that the designer of Central Park in New York had incorporated many of its features.

Jimmy's calculations proved correct, the park was full of families, groups of youths and girls, all enjoying the many facilities. Tennis courts, bowling greens and a cricket pitch provided healthy pursuits and as predicted there was a boating lake of exceptional design that gave the impression that the user was travelling along a winding river.

After a number of futile attempts to engage with groups of girls it was decided, democratically, Bill dissented, to hire a boat and put their seamen's skillson display. Jimmy took charge on the grounds that he was not only three months senior to the others but he had served on two ships, all be it that his first ship had only left port once whilst he was a member of the crew.

Jack and Bill were assigned to the oars, Jimmy took the tiller and Ronnie took station in the prowto act as lookout for any likely lasses who may require the aid of seasoned seafarers. Compared to the civilians already afloat their handling of the small craft was in a different category. The timing of the rowers and their easing off and laying on of the oars enabled them to manoeuvre with little application of the tiller. With no effort they sped across the water at a pace that irritated other rowers, particularly youths of similar age and their accomplishmentdrew glances of admiration from the females and looks of envy from the males.

"I'm getting hungry,"Ronnie said.

"I don't know why cos you ain't done anything," Bill retorted.

"I'll 'ave no bickering in the lower decks,"Jimmy pushed the tiller over, "ice cream stall over there, who fancies one?"

"I fancy one o' those lasses sat on the grass,"Ronnie leered at three girls sunning themselves a few yards from the stall.

"They look like nice, decent girls," Bill did not seem amused by Ronnie's lustfulness.

"Oh, well I'll stay clear o' them, mon, I prefer the other type. What about you Jimmy?"

Jack sensed Bills discomfort, "Let's keep going, there was another stall by where we got boat," he suggested in an effort to ease the situation, 'an' it looked nicer than this one."

But Ronnie was already reaching out with the boat hook and drawing the vessel into the bank and Jimmy was on his feet with the rope in his hand. Before Jack could repeat his suggestion Jimmy leapt ashore and began securing the rear of craft to a small sapling,Ronnie then did the same with the prow and then they both headed for the girls leaving Jack and Bill to lay in the oars. Ronnie and Jimmy had already seated themselves on the grass beside the girls and had engaged them in conversation as the other two made their way up the low bank.

"Where are you from?" a small dark haired girl with a bad complexion askedRonnie.

"Newcastle," he replied proudly as he always did when talking about his hometown, "I'm a Geordie."

"Can we buy you girls an ice cream?"Jimmy askedgallantly getting to his feet expecting his offer to be accepted.

"No thanks," a girl with thick brown hair answered for all of them. She appeared to be a little older than the others and neither of them contradicted her decision, "we've already had one."

"Well another wouldn't hurt," Jimmy insisted, "you've got four handsome sailors here to spend the afternoon with, what could be better?"

"What are your names?"Ronnie asked.

The girls obliged, the older one was called Anne, the dark one Kath and the third Mary.

"Is it true that sailors have a girl in every port?" Anne asked her manner softening a little.

"That's a fact," Jimmy agreed, "but none as lovely as you."

"Listen to him," Mary scoffed, "you're a real jack-the-lad, you aren't you."

"Haven't you got a girlfriend waiting for you?" Anne directed her question at Ronnie.

Throughout the brief, and futile, exchange Bill and Jack had sat a little apart, neither of them eager to become involved. When Ronnie answered Jack had to restrain his friend.

"Not me," he laughed, "I'm single and available."

Bill went to get to his feet, his face black with anger but Jack laid a restraining hand on his shoulder.

"Did you hear what he said," he seethed, "Amy writes to him twice a week."

The efforts of Jimmy and Ronnie came to nothing and after ten minutes the girls left, deaf to their pleadings. As they returned to their boat Bill tackled Ronnie over his intended betrayal of Amy.

"Why did you say you ain't got a girl," he demanded angrily, "I thought you were keen on our Amy?"

"Yeah,"Ronnie agreed, "Amy's alright..."

"What d'you mean, alright?" his anger grew, "she writes to you and..."

"Bill,"Ronnie's joviality left him, "Amy is just using me to get at Jack," he looked across at Jack for confirmation, "ain't that right Jack?"

"Amy wouldn't do that," even as he spoke Bill knew that he had always known this to be the truth but he couldn't admit it now, he had to protect his sister as though she were at his side. He suddenly underwent a surge in his maturity. The sister, with whom he had spent all of his life in infantile conflict now, in some miraculous transformation, seemed to need his masculine protection. This realisation of a new rapport with her did nothing to temper his anger. "You take that back, Raven," he was shouting now, and passing people cast wary looks at a group sailors arguing.

"Jack, you know I'm right, will yer tell 'im."Ronnie begged.

Jack knew that Ronnie was stating a fact, even Lil had seen through Amy's ploy, but he was in a difficult position. If he supported either he would alienate the other. He knew what the truth was, but truth or lie he would have to take a side. While he still struggled with his dilemma Bill's next action removedthe need for him to commit himself.

Exasperated or embarrassed,Ronnie decided to end the dispute by walking away; he turned and headed for the boat. In Bills eyes this was not the best course to resolve their difference over Amy and rather than pouring oil on water it was more akin to throwing oil onto a fire, Bill blew up. The push in the back of the retreating Ronnie was meant to be violent but the energy that he calculated would be sufficient revenge was exaggerated by Ronnie's momentum and the slope. The result was that Ronnie hurtled down the incline towards the lake the only obstacle in his way being Jimmy, who at that moment was bending over to untie the rope that secured the boat. His muscular bulk saved Ronnie from a ducking but sadly Ronnie's impact with his behind drove him head first into the murky water.

The angry exchange ended abruptly, groups of people paused and gazed upon the scene with an air of apprehension and profound interest. A youth began to laugh but the tension of the situation reached him and he stoppedinstantly, it seemed that even the birds stopped singing. Jack, Bill and Ronnie stood open mouthed, waiting for the storm.

Jimmy, waist deep in the lake with his thick black hair matted to his head, calmly recovered his cap, which floated nearby, and began to wade slowly to the shore, his head bowed and silent. Neither threat norcurse passed his lips as he slowly climbed from the water and stood dripping on the grassy bank. The three of them tensed still expecting an eruption.

He eventually looked up from examining his condition, "Who did it?" he spoke quietly but his anger was evident. When Bill and Ronnie both started talking at once, his control snapped, "Shut up," he screamed. Onlookers turned away or moved on. Jimmy poked a thick finger at Ronnie and moved further up the bank, "was it you?"

Ronnie wisely retreated, his hands held up in supplication, "He pushed me, Jimmy," he pointed at Bill.

"Yeah," Bill admitted, following Ronnie's example and backing away, "but I didn't mean to...it was...he was being 'orrible about Amy," he moved further away.

"I'm gonna batter both of yer," he made a dash at Ronnie who was the nearest, but spurred on by terror and having the advantage of being higher up the slope Ronnie easily escaped. Jimmy turned his attention to Bill who, having the same assistance and impetus as Ronnie, was also able to distance himself quickly from the Scouse destroyer.

"Don't look at me," Jack objected as Jimmy looked around like a wounded bear, breathing heavily and scowling, "I had nothing to do..." his protest was cut short as Jimmy grabbed him roughly by the front of his tunic.

"You were with 'em," Jimmy growled and raised a ham like fist.

The punch never landed, "Cook!" the voice boomed out like the arrival of a hundred pound shell and had exactly the same effect on Jimmy, and he froze

124

in an image of grace and aggression. The Regulator who had booked them off the ship and a beefy Petty Officer looked down on the scene like two avenging angels.

The single word was enough, Jimmy's ferocity turned to mercy. He released Jack and smoothed the creases from his tunic, "Just a little misunderstanding, skipper,"he explained, "we..."

"How the bloody hell did you get into that state?" The PO bawled. The few civilians that had stayed to observe now left, hurriedly.

"Accident, Sir."

"You're one bloody great accident, Cook," the PO retorted, "get yourself back to the ship now before you cause the Navy any more embarrassment," he turned to two more members of the shore patrol who arrived on the scene, "Mason, take this individual back and don't let him get into any more trouble."

Earlier than was required Jack returned to the ship alone, Ronnie and Bill had made themselves scarce on the arrival of the shore patrol and neither of them was eager to meet up with Jimmy again until he had calmed down or there were plenty of witnesses around to make it less likely that murder would be committed. Jack descended the ladder into the mess with a fair degree of caution and apprehension. Jimmy was in his hammock reading a *penny dreadful* and attired only in his underwear.

"You might well creep in, Cornwell," he lowered the comic and looked at Jack, "you and your bloody mates."

"Hey, Jimmy, come on. I had nothing to do with that," Jack pleaded.

"Which one of 'em did it?"

Jack grimaced, "I can't snitch on a mate Jimmy, you wouldn't really want me to, would yer?"

"I thought I was a mate?" Jimmy swung himself of the hammock and tested the dryness of his uniform that was hanging over one of the many pipes that crisscrossed the ceiling of the mess.

"Yeah, you are," Jack half agreed, "but the others are a bit scared of you..."

"And you're not?" Jimmy pulled his tunic off the pipe satisfied with its condition.

"Maybe,"

"Only, maybe?"

"Me dad always told me not to show when yer scared," Jack explained as he slung his own hammock, 'cos the other fellah might be more frightened than you are and back down, but if 'e knows you're scared 'e won't."

"Well I'm not backing down kidder." Jimmy grinned.

"An' I ain't showing you I scared." Jack returned the grin.

Jimmy tousled Jacks hair, "Good lad."

*

Ships log, Monday 15th of May. 0930 work up main engines, 1000 commence full speed trials. 1100 gunlayer, Sight-Setter and trainer to .303 aiming practice at towed targets.

"Take the first pressure, deep breath, let half out and squeeze the trigger. Don't snatch."The Royal Marine Lance Corporal stood behind the three marksmen as they took aim with their Lee Enfield's at targets, fixed to buoys, that were being towed behind the ship, "Raven, you bloody moron hit the sodding target and leave the buoy afloat."

Although the targets were a mere hundred yards away the motion of the ship combined with the more extreme activity of the buoys, as they bounced along in the ships wake, made the targets a challenging proposition.

*

Ships log, Tuesday 16th of May. 0800 left port. 0900 Gunnery ratings to drill,torpedo parties prepare torpedoes.

The GO's voice was loud and clear, much to Jacks relief. He had feared that the howling wind and noise of the bow crashing through the waves, combined with the static problem they had experienced the previous day would have caused some difficulty.

"Ready!" he repeated the GO's order.

Peter Lawless slammed the breech shut, "Ready!" he repeated.

WS placed his finger on the trigger and waited. Alf Tucker and Art Furby took up a new shell and charge respectively, and waited.

Jacks heart pounded with the excitement. The GO's voice, Jack repeats, "Fire!"

The gun roared, WS removed his hand from the trigger, Peter snatched open the breech and smoked flowed out as Alf Tucker rammed home the shell followed by the charge from Art, Peter slammed the breech closed again.

"Ready!"

Jack, "Ready!" His heart swelled with pride at the fact that he was part of this efficient team who trusted and relied on each other. WS looked across at him and seemed sense Jacks elation, he winked and gave him a thumbs-up. Jack sighed deeply content with his lot.

The only fly in the ointment, the issue that marred this perfect life, was the relationship between Ronnie and Bill. They had not spoken to each other since their run ashore in Birkenhead. Jimmy had soon forgotten the ducking and was on the same terms with all of them that had existed since their days at *Vivid*. Both Ronnie and Bill were being stubborn and neither would agree to reconciliation. Jack found the situation both frustrating and disheartening, they were his friends and he wanted to share this wonderful bond of comradeship with both of them, but if he was chatting on the mess deck with one and the other appeared then the first departed. He longed for the state of affairs that had existed throughout their training.

Chapter Eleven

Ships log Tuesday the 16ᵗʰ of May. 1725, came to with port anchor at Scapa Flow.

They had joined the British Grand Fleet; the sight wasspectacular. Twenty-four battleships, three battle cruisers, thirty destroyers and dozens of light scouting cruisers, lay at anchor with the sun slipping below the low hills to the west, washing the gathered might of the most powerful navy in the world in a gentle light that diminished their hostile aura. The clear evening sky was blemished with a hundred thin columns of grey smoke that rose from the silent fleet. Screaming seagulls floated over the grey monsters alert for waste buckets being emptied over the sides.

HMS *Chester* had come to anchor in a bay on the south side of the small village of Whome. To arrive at her anchorage she had to make her way through a good part of the fleet. The sense of power that Jack had been experiencing over the past weeks as HMS*Chester* sped across the North Sea displaying her speed and armour, now left him. Compared to the mighty vessels scattered around the Flow, *Chester* now seemed quite insignificant.

"Aye, lad," WS replied when he mentioned this, "but we have speed on our side. That's what our job is, we scout ahead of the fleet and we can run away if the odds is agin us."

Jack felt a little of his confidence return.

Ships log Tuesday 23ʳᵈ of May. 0800 weighed anchor and proceeded to sea for battle practice.
0940 exercise General Quarters.

The klaxon had become part of their everyday life but this did not mean that the response was any the lessurgent than the first time it had set the adrenaline pumping. Reaction to the alarm was a matter of survival, whether it be a fire or enemy presence, the crew's speed of action was essential to the safety of the ship. There was no possibility of retreat from a warship, it was simple, if the ship was destroyed then the crew had little chance of survival.

Standing at his battle station, his gun, Jack reflected on the week that had passed since their arrival at Scapa Flow. He had never worked so hard in his life as the crew and ship worked up in preparation for the inevitable clash with the Kaiser's Imperial Fleet. Both sides knew that it was a confrontation that had to take place for either adversary to have any chance of victory. If Germany could overcome the might of the Royal Navy then Britain could be starved into submission. It was conflict that both sides knew that they must win.But this was for political and military leaders to concern themselves over, for most participants at the lower end of the command chain it was the day-by-day and hour-by-hour continued existence that occupied their attention andlabour.

The training programme was intense and enduring; battle practice was made as realistic as could be. Sleep was taken when the chance was offered but it was never extensive and the sleepthat they did get was invariably interrupted. Sleep deprivation was a serious issue, men had to be driven and tempers became frayed it was not an ideal time or situation for Ronnie and Bill to put an end to their differences. It still worried Jack and added to the pressures.

He was coping with demands of the battle preparation; he was the baby of the team and the rest of them watched over him like so many mother hens and his friendship with Jimmy was stronger. It annoyed him a little, when he expressed his worries over Bill and Ronnie, that Jimmy's attitude was so indifferent.

"Don't worry about 'em, you're still mates with both of 'em, let them sort it out."

"But they're my mates an' I can't chat to both of them together. If I'm chatting with Bill, Ronnie won't come near and the same if I'm with Ronnie."

"Hey," Jimmy poked him in the chest, "we've enough t' worry about our kid, just keeping on top of all this, I tell yer, I'm knackered."

The voice of the GO in his head set brought him back to the immediate task, "Range two-thousand,"

Jack repeated the order to the team and they went into action. Just over a mile away a destroyer was passing across their bow and a half a mile behind she towed a scrapped hulk, this was their target.

Ships log Thursday 25th of May. 0700 weighed anchor. 0800 Run torpedoes, 0900 hoisted torpedoes. 0925, aiming practice at moving target. 1140 dropped lifebuoy, exercised sea boats crew.

It was a little after midnight when Jack ended his tour of duty on the first watch and he climbed gratefully into his hammock, dog-tired. It had been a long day and a lot of the training had been physically hard but he had managed a few quiet moments after mess call to write some letters. It was a task that he had neglected over the past two weeks, not from lack of care but the sheer pressure on his time and the need for sleep, it was difficult to find the time, or concentrate.

On his way on watch he had deposited two letters in the Writers office, one to his mother and one to Romin. He had received a letter from his father the previous morning and felt guilty that he had not replied but made a promise to himself that he would rectify this omission the next day.He had reached that stage of fatigue when it was difficult to sleep and the grunts and snores of those around him did nothing to help him achieve unconsciousness. Earlier in the day, whilst he was waiting his turn in the sea boat he had been able to chat with Bill.

131

"I had a letter from Amy this morning," he told Jack, "she asked how you were."

"Oh!" Jack was surprised, "how is she?"

"She's alright; she was a bit upset about what Ronnie had said."

"You told her?" Jack said in disbelief.

"Yeah, why not," he replied with equal incredulity.

Jack shook his head, "It just seems daft, she didn't have to know."

"Course she did."

"It's bad you and Ronnie not being mates, Bill." Jack changed the subject.

"Well it's his fault," he stared down into the water.

"Maybe, but we're gonna be in the fight soon and what if one of us..." the sentence went unfinished; they were called forward by the coxswain.

*

Lil heard the snap of the letterbox just as she was sitting down to her breakfast. Letters were frequent in the Cornwell household, with Eli and two sons all serving there was at least a letter every other day.

She recognised the handwriting, "It's from Jack," waving the envelope above her head she ran out into the yard where her mother was feeding the chickens.

Lily wiped her hands on her apron, took the letter and returned to the kitchen opening it as she went. "Let's see what our sailor boy has to say."

"Come on Mum, I'll be late for school."

Lily sat down at the kitchen table and read aloud, "'Dear Mum, I was very glad to get your letter and hear that all is well as leaves me at present. I had a letter from dad yesterday and he says that his battalion has gone over to the Defence Corps, he doesn't seem very pleased.'Your dad must have written to him the same time he wrote to us. 'I hear conscription has

132

come out official but I hope they don't nab Ern. Tell Lil that I am sorry she could not get in the school she wanted but tell her not to get the rats. I am pretty sparing with writing today as we have had a hard day at sea and tonight I am on the first watch. I am pretty tired as you can bet and I will be glad when I can turn in. I will write more later. I remain your ever-loving son, Jack

PS. Remember me to all. XXXXX. Write again as soon as possible. XXXXX these kisses are for the chickens and cats. This is a lot of kisses to give away.'"

Lily slowly folded the letter and put it in her apron pocket.

"Why are you crying Mum? Jack's alright isn't he?"

"I dunno ducks, I just miss 'im so much," she dabbed her eyes.

"I do Mum,"she hugged her mother, "I miss Dad and Arthur too"

*

About the same time that Lily and Lil sat in the kitchen to read Jack's letter, Megan tapped lightly on the door of Romin's bedroom and then enteredwithout waiting for a reply, carrying a tray that contained a pot of tea and a boiled egg. She put the tray onto a small side table and opened the curtains. Romin was awake and lay watching her. Normally an early riser, she had taken to staying in bed late, and remaining in her room for most of the day. She looked tired and had lost weight.

Romin smiled, "There's a letter from Jack," she took it from the tray and handed it to her.

Romin sat up smiling, "Thank you, Megan. Have you heard from Nobby?"

"Not since Saturday, he's probably finding it difficult to write at the moment. Now please eat Miss Romin, you mustn't be ill."

"I will."

When Megan had left Romin used the knife from the tray to carefully slit upon the envelope. She read, *Dear Romin, I am sorry that I have not been able to write as often as I have done recently but we have been really busy working up the ship. We have left my last port and we have now joined other ships in the north. It's allfeeling very exciting but it's very hard work and we don't get much sleep. Ronnie and Bill have had a fall out and I am trying to sort it but they are as bad as each other. I am on watch at eight so I can't write much. I will write again soon and I hope I canmake it longer next time. Your friend, Jack. PS. I know your still in the dumps but keep writing,your letters keep me going.*

She read it through three more times, then, feeling a little better she ate the breakfast that Megan had brought her; that done she took a pad of writing paper from her dressing table drawer and sat down to write.

*

Ships log 18th of May Sunday. 0930 Blue and Red Watches to Divine Service on Fara

It had been a chilly start to the day but now the sun had broken through and dissolved the sea mist warming the backs of the blue multitude that gathered on the gentle, heather covered, slope. At the lower end, an altar of Royal Marine drums had been constructed and partly covered with the White Ensign and Union Flag. Immediately in front of the altar a double row of chairs were occupied by senior officers and behind them a mass of ratings extended up the slope. A Royal Marine band was formed up on the left of the altar. Lord Jellicoe was in attendance and the Chaplain from HMS *Iron Duke*, the Admirals flagship, conducted the service.Half way up the slope the elements from HMS *Chester* were grouped, a small part of the four thousand in attendance.

A southwesterly breeze, still bearing the coolness of the early morning, rolled in from the sea and carried the words of the Chaplain to the host as effectively as any Tannoy.

"As Our Lord has taught us, so lets us pray.' Four thousand voices delivered the Lord's Prayer to the empty blue sky, the wheeling seagulls and thesea strewn with vessels of war.

Jack was finding the service the most moving that he had ever attended. In the company of friends, friends who, had become as close as family, had shared hardships and laughter, and in a few days would share the terror and peril of battle, he now shared the peace of a religious service. He thought of his family who would at this time be attending the same rite in the same church that he had attended for most of his life. He thought of his father in similar company and also possibly on a church parade. And of his eldest brother, Arthur, with the Middlesex Regiment in France, of them all he was the least likely to have the comfort and peace of a Holy gathering to give him solace.

As was to be expected, the Chaplain likened the gathering before him to the parable of the feeding of the five thousand, "And unlike that multitude gathered on the hillside overlooking the Sea of Galilee, you will not witness a miracle with loaves and fishes, but instead you should be nourished with the Lords love and protection in the fight to come, safe in the knowledge that God is on our side and will fill you with the courage and dedication thatyou need to carry you through the Hell that is war. Our final hymn; *Eternal Father, Strong to Save.*"

The Bandmaster raised his baton and the opening bars of the 'sailors hymn' washed over the congregation provoking emotions from pride to humility. The voices were strong but many a tear ran down many a weather-beaten cheek;

'*Eternal Father, strong to save,*

135

Whose arm hath bound the restless wave,
Who biddest the mighty ocean deep,
Its own appointed limits keep,
Oh, hear us when we cry to thee,
For those in peril on the sea'

When the final notes were blown away across the barren hillsideAdmiral Lord Jellicoe took station before the altar. Silence descended; His Lordship stood quietly surveying Nelson's heirs and they in turn held the silence, waiting. It was a little over a century since the greatest of Britain's sailors sailed out to meet the challenge of another enemy, at Trafalgar. The battle that confronted his navy this day was no less crucial.

"In the coming days," he began,"you will confront an enemy of great might, skill, courage and resolve. These are qualities that I know youalso possess and in great measure. The trial that faces us is of immeasurable magnitude. Failure could represent defeat for our beloved nation, we, the Imperial Fleet, must defeat the Kaisers Grand Fleet or they will have a strangle hold on our country,"he paused to allow them time to ponder on his words."But I have every confidence that your resolve, courage and determination will last those critical moments longer than the enemy's and what is more important, in the approaching storm, is your sense of duty. The sense of duty to your messmates, your shipmates and most importantly your sense duty to your King and Country. We all depend upon each other. The ship's captain cannot sail his vessel without his crew and every member of the crew depends on the skills of his shipmates; everyone is essential from the stoker to the captain, we must all do our duty to defeat the enemy and protect our shipmates." He raised his plumed hat aloft, "God Save Great Britain and protect her from her enemies."

A mighty cheer went up that could be heard on the neighbouring isle's and every ship in the fleet, and thousands of hats rose into the air like an endless flight of startled birds.

Chapter Twelve

Ships log 31st of May Wednesday. 0500 Weighed anchor. 0600 turned 32 points to starboard to gain touch with armoured cruisers.

It had been an early reveille but before they had weighed anchor Jack had finished his letter to his father and managed, to his great relief, to get it on the last lighter to leave with the fleet's mail.

Ships log, 0930 exercised General Quarters. General course for forenoon, South, 50 degrees East. Manoeuvring with two-point zig-zag.

At General Quarters WS had them checking the gun and ammunition and ensuring the area was cleared away ready for action. HMS *Chester* and HMS *Canterbury* were running five miles ahead of Admiral Hoods 3rd Battle Cruiser Squadron, as light cruisers this was their role, scouting, they were fast and manoeuvrable.Visibility had been down to about three thousand yards for most of the morning and for most of this time *Chester* was a mile ahead of *Canterbury* so to all intents and purposes she was virtually alone.But as in all battles, the average soldier, or sailor, are completely ignorant of the whole picture, they are only witness to, and concerned with, the fight that goes on around them.

"Mark my words," Moses said, "if we runs into them buggers now, we're goners."

"You're a right gloom and doom merchant, Moses," Alf Tucker grinned.

"You won't be smiling, Alf Tucker, if a bloody great German battle ship comes steaming out of that fog wi' her ten inch guns a blazing."

"Rumour has it that they're still in port." WS said calmly.

"Oh, aye," Moses was not convinced, "then why are we out 'ere, two pointing like our lives depended on it?"

Further discussion was halted as the Tannoy called hands to stand down.Mugs of tea and thick slices of bread spread thickly with margarine and jam formed their midday meal.

This frugal repast again had Moses offering his disgruntled opinion, "If we was villains waiting for the hangman's rope we'd be dining like kings, enjoying the condemned man's last meal, an' look at what we've got," he slapped a thick slab of bread onto the table as a reply to his own question.

"You're not a condemned man, you moaning old sod," Art Furby pointed out.

"If we runs into the German fleet," Moses wagged a crust of bread to make his point, "we're all condemned men."

"Stow it Moses," WS snapped, "it's young Jacks first action an' you're putting the fear o' Christ in him."

"I'm alright," Jack wiped his mouth with the back of his hand and took a mouthful of tea."Can I go and see me mates, Corporal?"

"You can," WS pointed to a slice of bread in front of Jack, "but be sure to eat that, we don't when we'll get the chance to eat again."

Jack found Bill sitting on the step of a ladder reading a letter, "From your mum?" he asked.

Bill looked up, unsmiling, "Yeah."

"You pals with Ronnie yet?"

Bill shook his head and carefully put his letter into his tunic pocket, "Naw."

Jack sensed an air of indecision in Bills manner, "Have yer tried?"

He shook his head again and sighed, "I suppose I should, our Gun-Layer reckons we'll meet the Germans today and if not today then tomorrow," he looked at Jack sadly. "I suppose one of us could catch one."

Jack nodded, "I suppose."

*

On HMS *Chester*'s bridge Captain Robert Neale Lawson studied the charts with his navigation officer, Lt Ian Bladon, as other officers of the watch scanned the horizon with powerful binoculars.

"This is our position, Sir," Bladon pointed to a spot on the chart with the point of a pair of compasses, "and *Canterbury* is over here,"

"We'll maintain our present course and speed. I cannot believe that Hipper has remained in port." The Captain picked a pair of binoculars and joined those at the window. Another Lieutenant entered the bridge and saluted Lawson's back.

"Message from *Hood*, Sir," Peter Machin, the Signals Officer said.

"Read it Mr Machin," the Captain said without lowering his glasses.

Machin cleared his throat, "Message from Admiral Beatty..."

"Yes, yes, get to purpose of the signal." Lawson cut in irritably.

"Er, yes, Sir," he cleared his throat again, "*Galtea* and *Phaeton* have sighted enemy cruisers,*Canterbury* to take up position five miles east of battle squadron and *Chester* five miles west. Timed 1510, signal ends, Sir."

Lawson was already back at the chart, "Fix *Galtea* and *Phaeton*'s positions, Ian."

Bladon went to work with his instruments.

Ships log, 1516.Increased to full speed, alter course south 25 degrees west. Pass priority signal, hands to action stations.

As they dashed for the ladder the four boys came together, they all sensed that this was no longer training. They paused briefly at the bottom of the ladder.

Jimmy grabbed Jacks hand, "Good luck Jackie," he then shook hands with Bill and Ronnie in turn wishing them the same.

Jack's heart leapt when Bill took Ronnie's hand, "Good luck Ron,"

"And you, mon," Ronnie replied and smiled.

Bill suddenly grabbed Jack in a bear hug, "Look after yourself, mate."

"And you, Bill."

"Come on you bloody baby sailors, get out of the way." A big AB pushed Jack up the ladder.

Visibility had increased and now they could see another warship on the horizon out to their left.

"She looks like the *Canterbury*," Moses squinted.

"How far is she Moses?" WS asked.

"Good ten miles I'd guess."

"They must be thereabouts," Alf Tucker looked grimly round the gun shield.

HMS *Chester* cut through the grey sea at twenty-six knots making spray that covered the forecastlegun and the crew, drenching them. The tension gradually decreased as time passed. Over the next two hours the light cruiser changed course four times and reduced speed to twenty knots to conserve fuel. The noise of the wind and engines did not make conversation easy and little talk took place.

WS leaned across the breech of the gun and motioned Jack to come closer, he did so and lifted one side of his headset to hear what the marine corporal had to say, "How are you feeling lad,"

"Alright," Jack grinned to reinforce his words.

"When its starts, just concentrate on what you have to do, don't pay no heed to the noise. There's nought you can do about it anyway," Jack nodded, still grinning, "You'll be alright son," WS added and leaned across and patted him on the shoulder.

When they had taken post Jack had felt more nervous than at any time since joining the ship. The exchange with Bill, Jimmy and Ronnie had unsettled him; there was an ominous quality about the brief dialogue. This disquieting feeling had now past and he felt happy that Ronnie and Bill appeared to have resolved their difference. Admittedly, the emotion of the moment had affected them but at least there was a good prospect that things would return to normal between them.

From his position behind the shield he could see nothing and he faced the rest of the gun crew who huddled on each side of the breech chatting. Every so often he peered round the shield but the view did not change; a veil of fine spray through which the grey rolling North Sea could just be discerned.

The GO's voice in his headset startled him, "Enemy sighted."

"Enemy sighted," he shouted, the eight men moved to their positions calmly and waited.

Ships log, 1730 sighted gun flashes SSW altered course SSW. 1735, sighted hostile cruisers and two destroyers ahead(Frankfurt & Wiesbaden – cruisers Elbing & Pilau also cruisers)

"Look!" Harry Luxton pointed; four cruisers were heading towards them on their starboard lee.

"Them's Huns alright,"Moses adjusted his cap and placed his hand on a new charge.

"Projectile, load!" The GO's voice conveyed his excitement.

Jack, "Projectile load!" he turned the deflection scale to zero.

142

The shell and charge were rammed home and the breech slammed shut with a satisfying crash. The ship heeled as the port guns engaged the approaching enemy vessels. They had no time to watch for the fall of shot; Jack was passing the GO's orders.

"Range six thousand," handles turned and wheels spun and the guns barrel raised its menacing snout a few degrees. Another salvo crashed out from the port battery and Jack had to repeat the next order. "Deflection five knots."

Two shell bursts straddled their bow drowning them in spray.

"That's some shooting," Moses screamed above the din, "the bugger'll have us with the next one."

The GO's voice was barely audible;"Bearing...' the rest of the order was drowned by the noise.

"Say again, all after bearing," Jack was shouting.

Before the GO could answer a shell struck the superstructure behind the gun with a great metallic crash. The blast threw the entire gun crew to the deck and showered them with shrieking splinters of steel and choking smoke. The speed of the ship soon cleared most of the smoke revealing a scene of appalling damage and carnage. Of the nine men in the gun crew only four regained their feet. Moses lay motionless, face down in a pool of blood. Sitting close to Moses, with his back to the superstructure and just below where the shell had struck; Alf Tucker was trying to staunch the blood that pumped from his thigh, talking to the inert Moses, but the din obliterated his words. David James lay by the ships rail having been blown there by the blast. The remaining two crew members were not to be seen.

"You alright,lad?" WS hauled himself to his feet blood trickling from small cuts on his smoke blackened face. Peter Lawless and Harry Luxton were also up and like WS were suffering from minor wounds to their faces.

Jack nodded, too stunned to speak. He readjusted his headset and took post by the sights. Before he could fully gather his wits another salvo crashed into the fo'c'sle, one striking the bow in front of the gun and the other close to where Moses and Alf lay. Again they were all thrown to the deck but this time only Jack and Peter got to their feet. WS had been thrown against the gun shield, a piece of shrapnel the size of a large dinner plate embedded in his chest, his unblinking eyes wide with surprise.

Jack found it harder this time to regain his feet, his legs did not seem to be responding and when he pulled to hard with his arms he suffered sharp pains in his stomach and chest. Supporting himself on the guns breech Jack gazed numbly at the chaos that surrounded him. Peter was still alive but had sustained a wound to his shoulder and upper arm and remained sitting on the deck. Shells continued to rain on and around *Chester* but these strikes seemed be landing more towards aft.

Despite his sheltered position Jack had been affected by the spray thrown up by the shells that had landed in the sea, consequently he felt wet but the wetness increased and it was warm. There was a movement at the bottom of the gun shield that caught his eye and on looking down he saw Harry Luxton crawling from the front of the gun into the protection of the shield. His hands were covered in blood and he had a large open wound at the back of his head.

Jack reached down and helped him into cover, and excruciating pain shot through his body, "Here, get down under cover, Harry."

Harry slumped against the metal wall, "They've knocked us about a bit lad. Be a good lad and get me drink from yonder bucket."

Wooden buckets, filled with water or sand were placed behind each gun to put out fires that may

144

threaten the ammunition. Crouching, Jack crossed the few feet to the buckets; more pain shot up his legs and when he tried to lift it a spasm of red-hot needles seemed to be thrust into his body.

"Thanks, Jack," Harry took the ladle and drank deeply and then coughed violently.

Another shell shook the shattered cruiser and Jack supported himself on the gun. A voice crackled in his headset but the words were incoherent.

"Say again," he said into the mouthpiece.

"Range four thousand," the GO sounded breathless.

"All of the crews wounded, Sir," he winced, talking was painful.

"Is that Cornwell?"

"Sir."

"Everybody's injured?"

"Yes, Sir."

"Okay, Cornwell stay at your post you may be needed."

"Aye, aye, Sir."

Ships log, 1750 altered course to northeast and continued zig-zagging to avoid salvoes.

As the ship altered course, violently, Jack felt his feet slip on something greasy on the deck. He looked down and saw that he was standing in a pool of blood that was increasing in size as he looked. The pain from his stomach was like a fire that now gripped his whole being and he gritted his teeth to stop crying out as they bounced at full speed across the waves. Harry seemed to have passed out; his chin was sunk onto his chest and he was motionless. Jack felt a great tiredness sweeping over him and he longed to sink onto the deck next to his shipmate. He flinched as another shell hit the superstructure behind the gun and he could hear the shrapnel whistling viciously through the air about him.

The responsibility was almost bringing him to tears – he needed help. If the order came to fire he could manage the one round that was already loaded, all he had to do would be to lean across and snatch the trigger lanyard, but if the order came to fire again it would be beyond him; it would be an enormous task for a fully grown man of considerable strength and would take a long time but he was only a youth and small to boot, and the pain he was suffering every time he moved was becoming intolerable.

A surge of resolve filled him with some optimism when he thought about what his father had taught about the size of the dog in the fight and the fight in the dog. He could do it given time. To occupy his mind and forget the pain in his stomach he ran through the gun team's drill to load and fire.

*

"Mr Allen," Captain Lawson addressed his newest officer who was observing the enemy through binoculars.

"Sir," Charles Allen lower his binocular and faced his captain.

"Turn your glasses on the fo'c'sle gun." Charles did as he was ordered. "The crew seem to be badly mauled, what d'you see?"

"You're right, Sir. They all seem to be wounded, only the Sight-Setter appears to be on his feet and he seems to be in some distress, but he is still at his post."

"Plucky lad," the Captain turned his attention back to the command of his crippled ship.

*

Lord Jellicoe's words of the previous evening had inspired Jack. The words about duty to the team and to the ship, to be reliable and support each other.;some of the team were probably already dead – but he could not let his mind dwell on that possibility – but the wounded would think badly of him if he did not

146

do his duty in the true tradition of the service. He knew that he would not be able to face their disappointment in him if he failed in his duty, he was so proud of being accepted into their family.

He was beginning to feel faint.He leaned against the gun but the pressure on his side caused too much pain. He was wounded of that he was fully aware but he did not want to know the extent of his injuries, such knowledge may alarm him and weaken his resolve.

He tried to compose his next letter to Romin in his head but he was finding it hard to concentrate. He thought of home and what those he had left behind would be doing on a Wednesday evening, but itwas beyond his ability to focus.The pain was crawling all over him. It immersed his whole body in teeth clenching agony and it was driving all thoughts from his mind other than the need to lie down and succumb to its domination.

"Is the gun serviceable, Cornwell?" the GO's words were badly distorted with static.

"Dunno, Sir. It was hit."

"Right, hang on; I'll try to muster another crew."

"Aye, aye, Sir."

Jack felt something tug at his trouser leg, Harry was conscious, "Get down, Jack, it'll be safer and you look shot at."

Jack shook his head, "The GO said to stay at my post, he's gonna send another gun crew."

"Where the hell is 'e gonna get another team, and anyway, this bugger won't be firing again."

Jack supported himself on the breech, his faintness had become dizziness.He thought he heard Lil's voice, faintly, amid the bellowing guns but she was barely audible, it could have been a seagull calling but was it unlikely that gulls would have been foolish enough to remain in the vicinity with all of the noise and turmoil?A shiver ran down his spine as he remembered her words, her dream of him being alone and scared and trying not to be;of the fire and noise and being in a cabin. He felt himself shiver again, did his little sister have special powers.

Ships log 1809 Enemy altered course to port, ceased firing, took station astern of 3rd Battle Cruiser Squadron. Grand Fleet sighted.

When Jack opened his eyes the pain had subsided but was still very uncomfortable. He was covered with a blanket and below decks but exactly where he was not sure. The area was busy and when he looked to his left he could see others similarly covered, on the right the same. There was a strong smell of iodine and disinfectant and sound of muffled conversation and subdued moans.

He was feeling drowsy despite his discomfort and the fact that he had only just woken. He did not know how long he had been asleep but the desire to return to the arms of slumber was strong. There was no way of telling what time of day it was but he had the impression – he did not know why – that it was night. In the distance he could hear the sound of thunder or shellfire. He had no longing to find out for certain or to speak with those around him. In fact there was little conversation considering there about forty men laying in rows and the few ratingspassing quietly among them, were doubtless sick bay attendants.

The weariness that was upon him was great but he was disappointed to realise that he was totally disinterested as to what was happening or how he had got where he was. Furthermore, he did not want to know what his injuries were, he asked himself if this was a sign of cowardice. He felt a gentle touch to his shoulder, he opened his eyes, and Jimmy and Bill were crouching at his side.

Jimmy blessed him with one of his infectious grins, "What you'll do to get out of doing yer watch, Cornwell," he took Jacks hand, "how are yer feeling, mate?"

"I'm alright now."

Bill edged forward, "Wotcha, mate," they both looked filthy and Bill was red eyed as though he had been crying.

"Where's Ronnie?" Jack asked straining his neck to spot him, the effort caused pain and he winced and lay back.

"The SBA says you got wounded in the stomach and legs," Bill said, "D'you want me to write to your mum?"

Jack smiled, "Would you? Just a quick line to tell her I'm alright," seeing his friends and speaking created an interest in the recent battle, "How did we go on?"

"What," Jimmy asked, "the fight?" Jack nodded, "well we lost a few ships and we've taken a bit of a beating, but the Germans broke off contact," he cocked his head and listened, "but there's still a fight going on over to the east."

"You didn't get hurt then?" he addressed both of them and winced again with the effort of speaking.

"Not us, but a few shells came pretty close, didn't they, Bill." Bill nodded, he seemed very subdued.

Jack asked the question he had asked earlier, dreading the answer, "How's Ronnie?" Bill's chin sank to his chest and his shoulders shook, Jack looked fearfully at Jimmy, "he ain't...?" He could not finish the question.

Jimmy gave a huge sigh, and took Jacks hand again, "Poor Ronnie..." his voice caught, and he started again, "Ronnie was killed, Jack," he bit his lip and Bill began to cry softly.

Jack shook his head, numbed by the news even though he had expected it, "No," he shouted, "not poor Ronnie," he began to sob, "He had no family, no one's gonna cry for 'im except us, poor, Ron." He covered his face with his hands.He coughed and blood ran down his chin.

The other two knelt in silence, helpless.

Bill leaned forward and touched Jacks hands, "I'm glad..., I'm glad you got us to be mates again, Jack."

An SBA came over to them attracted by Jacks shout. "You'll have to leave lads, he's got to rest," he guided them to the door. "He's very poorly," he told them when they were out of earshot of Jack.

"How bad is he?"Bill was fearful of the reply, "he doesn't seem too bad."

"Well he is, mate, multiple leg and stomach wounds and internal bleeding. There's not much we can do. We'll be in Immingham tomorrow sometime, and the wounded will go to Hull hospital, but the MO doesn't think your mate will last that long, he's lost a hell of a lot of blood."

Bill put his head on his arms and leaned against the bulkhead, great sobs wracked his body. Jimmy stood with a hand on his shoulder unashamed of this display of grief. A lot of tears were shed that night throughout the Grand Fleet. The final death toll was 6,197 with 510 wounded, and this was a battle won.

Ships log 2100 took station astern of the second cruiser squadron, course and speed as required to remain on station. Darkened ship.

Chapter Thirteen

Ships log Tuesday 1ˢᵗ of June. 0600 Hands employed, refitting, re rigging and cleaning upper deck.

Still filthy and unwashed from the previous days fight, scores of tired ratings faced the horrific task of clearing and cleaning HMS*Chester*'s battle-scarred deck. She had been hit by seventeen shells, the devastation was colossal. There were a number of large holes in the upper deck surrounded by debris; machinery was destroyed, side plates bent and holed and the fore bridge virtually destroyed.

Bill and Jimmy were in the party clearing the forecastle, one of the worst hit areas. The gun shield was badly damaged but not holed, but the machinery behind the gun and the superstructurehad taken two hits and it was these shells that had decimated the gun crew. The toll was now known; WS, Harry Luxton, Alf Tucker, Art Furby and Moses had all been killed. Peter Lawless had lost a leg, Davey James had severe chest wounds George Spillet had head wounds and was blind.

Jimmy made sure that Bill stayed well away from the immediate area of the gun. The inside of the shield, where Jack had been standing, had been peppered by steel splinters; Jimmy was amazed that Jack had survived at all. All around the area large patches of drying blood had to be swabbed away with buckets of seawater. As he mopped the deck, Jimmy did something that had not done since his childhood, he said a silent prayer for his plucky little friend and his secret tears mingled with his sweat.

Ships log 1040 Slow both engines. Committed to the deep the bodies of officers and men killed in action. Position, Latitude54 degrees 35N Longitude 0degrees 51E

Everyone had made some effort to smarten their soiled and torn uniforms and they gathered in double ranksamidships, on the port side. Fifteen bodies, sewn into their hammocks and draped in the Union Flag, lay on boards along the ships side and another fifteen lay in a row to one side. The service was short but respectful as is the practice of the services. After prayers led by the chaplain from HMS *Falmouth*;HMS*Chester*'s chaplain, Ambrose Walton, was among the dead, and the hymn *Abide with Me*. Captain Lawson made a moving speech about the courage and sacrifice of those who had died and the pain of losing shipmates; the boards were tilted and the bodies slipped into the grey sea.

Ships log 1710, arrived Immingham docks, pilot came on board, warped into lock. 1745 Secured in lock – landed wounded.

Jimmy had managed to get himself and Bill into the party that were detailed to carry the wounded ashore. There were thirty injured with varying degrees of injury but a large proportion had suffered wounds from splinters of shrapnel and burns. The transference was not an easy task and no matter how careful the stretcher-bearers were in handling their charges, pain was suffered.They had to be manhandled down the gangway and then across the dockyard; a distance of nearly a quarter of a mile, and onto the waiting trams at the dockyard gate. Wheeling them on improvised carts was out of the question in view of the yard being cobbled.For the duration of the move an eerie hush hung over the area, the wounded bore their pain with stoic silence and the dockworkers watched the distressing procession in a respectful hush.

At the gate the column of stretchers was greeted withapplause, whichwas polite but deep felt, from a few score civilians who had gathered when the news of HMS *Chester*'s arrival had spread through the town. Women, many of them in tears, detached themselves from the small crowd and placed flowers on the chests of the injured men,

Twice they had been forced to rest on the journey from the ship to the tram. Sturdy though Bill was, it was a long way to carry another human of equal weight.

"You're a waste of rations, Asher;" Jimmy told him, unsympathetically, "my little sister would 'ave been more bloody help."

"My bleeding arms are 'anging out of their sockets," Bill rubbed his arms, "I'll have arms like a chimp."

"Well yer've got a gob like one, so yer'll be alright."

Jack was drowsy from the effects of morphine but was conscious enough to hear and follow the banter of his friends and he wore a smile, feeling the urge to join in but neither having the words or the strength to utter them.He enjoyed hearing them, it was comforting, and he was back in the bosom of his family.His concern about his condition was briefly replaced by the warmth he felt surrounded by his friends.

"Easy now," Jimmy instructed as they eased the stretcher through the tram door and laid it gently on the wooden seat. "Where are they taking him, mate?" he asked of the SBA who was accompanying the wounded.

"Grimsby, Hospital."

"D'you hear that, Jack?" he leant closer, "Grimsby Hospital, if we get some shore leave I'll come down t'see yer."

"And I'll write to your mum, mate," Bill added as the SBA ushered them from the tram.

The members of hospital staff were doing their best to cope but the numbers arriving almostoverwhelmed them. There was no possibility that every patient could be allocated a bed and initial treatment and assessment was carried out in the corridors and reception area. The performance and dedication of the staff was exceptional and every one of the wounded had been examined by a doctor and had their dressings changed, where necessary, before ten o'clock.

Jack had been examined by a young naval medical officer, one of the six sent up to Grimsby from Portsmouth that morning. Lt Frasier Russell was competent but inexperienced but he was aware that Jacks wounds, though not the most horrific to observe, were grave and life threatening. He watched the nurse apply temporary dressings to his legs; an operation would be required to remove the scores of metal shards embedded there.

"Shall I put a dressing on his abdomen, Sir?" she asked.

Frasier continued examining the small punctures oozing blood, which covered Jacks torso from his groin to his lower chest, "Not at the moment, nurse, I want Commander Stephenson to see them. Matron is looking for him."

Surgeon Commander CS Stephenson was one of the seconded doctors and because of his wide knowledge of the type of wounds created by modern warfare he had overall command of the emergency.Before Nurse Dove had completed her task the Commander swept along the corridor accompanied by the formidable figure of Matron MavisRastall, feared, loved and respected in equal measure by her nurses and the junior doctors.

"This is the boy?" the Commander bent over Jack.

"I thought that he would require urgent surgery, Sir." Frasier offered.

"Quite so," the Commander agreed, and then to Jack, "have you had anything to drink?"

154

"No, Sir," Jack shook his head, "but I'm thirsty."

Commander Stephenson smiled and patted his shoulder, "I am afraid you will have to hang on a little longer." He turned to the nurse, "Has he coughed up any blood, nurse?"

"Quite a bit, Sir."

The Commander motioned Charles and Matron to follow and moved a few paces away and then continued in subdued tones,"This lad has severe internal bleeding, but I would think that he has a good chance of survival,although the operation will be intricate and prolonged," he paused and shot a pitying glance in Jack's direction, "But the truth is we do not have sufficient staff to perform such surgery at this time," he sighed deeply."Furthermore, there's is no certainty that he would survive it,and therefore I must reluctantly put him to the back of the queue in order to save those that I know can be saved." He paused again and clasped his hands,"From what I have seen thus far, we should have completed most operations by this time tomorrow, regardless, I will do this lad tomorrow evening if he can just hang on until then. Matron, would you be so kind as to send someone with a message to my secretary, Miss Broom, she can be found at reception, and would you detail a competent nurse to sit with him throughout the night."

Mary Broom loved her work; she had been employed as the Commanders secretary and driver since the second week of the war. This was her way of contributing to the war effort without going against her father's wishes. Stanley David Broom had not forbidden his daughter to take up nursing, as she had wished, but he had pleaded with her to seek other avenues in her effort to play her part in the war. His description of the negative aspects of nursing, of which he had first-hand knowledge as a surgeon, had not persuaded her but her respect for his wishes and the

155

offer of her present position had meant that they were both satisfied. Stanley knew that she would not have to suffer the full rigours and horrors of nursing badly maimed young men, and she was fulfilled in that she was able to assist a man of the Commanders skill by making the administrative side of his work less burdensome.

Mary was neat and precise in her appearance and all that she did and within ten minutes of receiving the Commanders instructions she had traced the young sailor's records and was dictating a telegram over the telephoneto be sent to his mother.It read: *Mrs L Cornwell. Your son, Boy First Class J42563 John Travers Cornwell is wounded. In Grimsby Hospital. Would advise you attend soonest. All expenses for you and one other will be reimbursed. Surgeon Commander Stephenson.*

*

The ward contained forty beds all of which were occupied by casualties of the recent great sea battle. At one end a single bed was curtained off and the light of a small oil lamp gave the small cubicle a cosy aura.

Matron Rastall, in hushed tones,was giving final instructions to the young nurse, "He is not to have any water other than a wet cloth on his lips," Lillian nodded. "He should not need any more sedative for a few more hours but call me if he appears to be suffering any distress."

Lillian nodded again, "Yes, matron."

"We must do our best for this little chap, nurse. If we can help him through the next few hours, he may be saved."Lillian, like the rest of the staff, feared and respected Mavis Rastall, but now she saw a soft motherly love in the older woman's tired eyes.

Lillian sat down on the chair facing Jacks bed and leaned forward so that the weak light from the lamp fell on her book. As the daughter of a clergyman she knew the Bible well and quickly found the page that she was looking for; James 5, verse 10.

She read aloud but softly hoping that the words would reach her patient, *"Brothers, as an example of patience in the face of suffering, take the prophets who spake in the name of the Lord. As ye know, we consider blessed those who have persevered..."*

"Is that the Bible?"

Lillian looked up from the page and found Jack awake and looking at her, his grey blue eyes clouded by the morphine.

"Yes," she leaned forward and touched his cheek, "do you read the Bible, Jack?"

"I go to church an' I used to go to Sunday school when I was a kid," his voice was hoarse and weak.

"Would you like me to wet your lips?"

"Can I 'ave a drink?"

"Sorry, Jack, I can only wet your lips."

"Why?"

"You have a stomach wound and liquids would be harmful," she placed a wet sponge on his mouth and allowed him to briefly suck on it.

"Where am I?"

"Grimsby Hospital, you were brought in this afternoon."

"What day is it?" his voice was getting weaker.

"Tuesday."

"So the battle was yesterday,"

She nodded.

His eyes filled, "My mate Ronnie's dead," he began to cry softly but the act caused him pain, he winced and screwed up his eyes.

"Oh, Jack I am so sorry," she wiped his tears away.

When he had stopped crying and the pain had subsided, he said, "You believe in God...sorry I don't know your name."

157

"Lillian, Lillian Dove."

He brightened a little, "My mum's called Lillian, but everyone calls her Lily, and so is my little sister, but we call her Lil."

"That must avoid any confusion," Lillian smiled, "and yes, I do believe in God," she tapped the Bible on her lap, "my father is the vicar of Waltham. I hope you believe, Jack."

He thought for a moment and sighed, "I suppose I still do, but he gave poor Ronnie a bad deal, he was a poor orphan and then he lets 'im get killed when he's just a kid."

"Man killed him, Jack, not God."

"Will you say a prayer for him please, Lillian?"

"We can both pray for him, Jack," she lowered her head and Jack closed his eyes."Lord hear our prayer for Ronnie who has died. As you have made us in your image and likeness and have called us by name, hold Ronnie safely in your love, in your kingdom of light, happiness and peace. Amen."

Jack repeated, "Amen," he reached out and touched her clasped hands, "Thank you."

*

Maude opened the door and her heart stopped. The telegraph boy was about Jacks age and of similar build but he was blond and wore glasses.

"Telegram for Missus Cornwell," he held out the yellow envelope.

"Mum!" Maude called over her shoulder, reluctant to take the missive.

"What is it?" Lily came to the door; there was fear in the question. When she saw the boy she gave a strangled cry and ran back into the house.

"Will there be a reply?" the boy asked unmoved by the event. He had delivered so many messages of grief that he was now unaffected by the heartbreak he witnessed almost daily.

Maude took the envelope and tore it open; hope filled her heart as she read the brief message, "No!" she said in answer to his question and closed the door.

Her mother was sat at the table when Maude returned to the kitchen, her face grey, "Who?" was all she could say.

Maude put her arm round Lily's shoulder, "Now it's not too bad,Mum,it's Jack, he's been wounded."

"What happened?" Lily grabbed the telegram from her daughter,"They want me to go up to Grimsby; it must be bad, what will it cost, where is Grimsby?"

Maude calmed her mother, "Take it easy Mum."

"Take it easy! How can I take it easy, my boy's dying and I don't even know where he is."

"Now make yourself a cup of tea and sit down, I've got some money and I'll go and see Bill's dad, he'll help us."

Thomas Asher not only loaned them the fare to Grimsby but he also paid for a cab to take them to the station and Sarah insisted that Lil and George stay at the Asher's until their mother returned from her desperate journey. As Lily and Maude sped on their way to St Pancras Station, the Asher's and the two Cornwell children knelt in prayer.

The eleven-twenty to Grimsby was packed to the doors; every compartment was full as the two women walked quickly up the platform growing more desperate with every carriage that they passed. Eventually, in the carriage next to the engine, they spotted a couple of vacant seats. The compartment was occupied by sailors on their way north as replacements for those lost in the previous day's engagement.

When the young men discovered the purpose of Maude and Lily's journey the two women were treated like royalty. Most of the men had newspapers that were full of reports of the great sea battle and they read out the more positive aspects of the devastating exchange, carefully avoiding any mention of the Grand Fleets terrible losses, both in ships and men.

Chapter Fourteen

The ward was in darkness apart from the faint light that shone dimly in the curtained bay. The silence was occasionally broken by whispered exchanges or groans of pain from those unable to achieve the solace of sleep. In other parts of the hospital the air of urgency still persisted as the fight to save lives went on but those in Ward 10 had received all the treatment available and were now in the hands of the nurses and God.

Jack had slept quietly for the last two hours and Lillian kept checking his pulse ever fearful that he had slipped away in his sleep. It was her task to nurse him through these critical hours until he could receive the attention of the surgeons. She prayed constantly for his deliverance.In the brief time that she had spent with him and the few words that they had exchanged she had recognised his quiet, undemonstrative courage and his deep love for his family and friends.

He coughed and blood spattered the sheet that was pulled up to his chin. As Lillian gently wiped his mouth and chin clean he opened his eyes.

"Mum?" his eyes were clouded with pain.

"No, it's me, Lillian, your nurse."

"Can I have a drink please?"

She dipped a sponge in water and wet his lips, "Is that better?"

"I hurt."

"Just a minute," Lillian pulled the curtain aside and signalled the nurse sitting in a pool of light by the door, "Call matron, quickly." She turned back to her patient knowing she had to try and take his mind off his agony, "You must tell me about the great fight you had with the Germans, Jack," she smiled encouragingly, not really wanting to hear the detail, seeing the results were sufficient.

He sighed and returned her smile modestly, "Oh, I think we carried on alright."

"Matron is on her way with a painkiller for you."

He looked at her steadily, in silence, for a moment, "I'm not frightened now," he gritted his teeth and shut his eyes tightly and then opened them. The sadness had gone and it was replaced with calm resignation, "Give my mother my love, I know she's coming," his eyes closed again and his body, and face relaxed in death.

Lillian, with tears streaming down her face, frantically checked his heart and felt for a pulse in his neck, knowing the truth but not wanting to accept it. She sank to her knees and surrendered to her grief.

"Nurse," matron came through the curtains, "take a hold of yourself."

"He's dead, matron," Lillian sobbed.

"And you're a nurse," matron checked Jack's body for signs of life, "act like one." Satisfied that there was nothing to be done for Jack she pulled the sheet up over his face and then took Lillian by the arm and led her out into the ward. "This is something you'll have get used to," her tone was softer, "it is sad to lose one so young, but all of these young men need our help, we can't let our emotions get the better of us."

Lillian dabbed her eyes and nodded, "I'm sorry matron, I must try to be as brave as he was."

"That's the spirit," matron patted her shoulder, "report to Sister Penn, she is short of staff."

As the young nurse walked dejectedly away matron dabbed her eyes with the corner of her handkerchief, sighed, and then with her head held high she went off to the next scene of tragedy.

*

He was conscious only of warmth, peace and utter contentment. The bright golden light at the end of the tunnel was welcoming and the darkness of the tunnelheld no fear. He was moving swiftly towards the light without any effort on his own part, it was as though he was floating.As he got closer to the brightness he could discern the shadowy figure of a human form, the detail of its dress and its features were obliterated by the light, which was behind it; but still he felt no fear. As he burst forth into the brilliance the figure threw out its arms in a gesture of greeting and at the same time its identity was revealed.

"I knew you were coming, mon," Reggie wore his lopsided grin as he clutched Jack to his thin chest.

Jacks first encounter with death had been when his paternal grandfather had died. His grandmother had tried to explain the unavoidable conclusion for all life, as best she could, to a sad little boy of six.

"But where's that?" Jack had asked when his Gran had told him that his grandfather's soul had gone to Heaven.

The old lady pointed skyward, "Up there, in the sky."

"But won't he be scared, up there, all on his own?"

She shook her head smiling, "No dear, when you arrive in Heaven, somebody who you knew and loved here on Earth and who has already died; will be there to greet you."

*

The early morning sun flooded the ward with light and warmth, a few walking wounded went about their ablutions or helped the staff to attend to the needs of those confined to their beds. The brightness of the day and relief of those who were glad to have survived the battle was restrained by the heart-rending act of mourning being conducted behind the screens at the end of the ward.

Maude sat at the bedside holding Jacks hand, a hand that was cold in death, her tears exhausted but her eyes swollen and red as evidence of their shedding. Lily was sat upon the bed, her body twisted round and laying across her dead son. Her shoulder shook with sobs that were now silent.

"He looks so peaceful, Mum." Maude lovingly stroked an errant strand of hair from his brow. Lily could only nod. Maude continued, 'even beautiful,' she laughed, "Imagine what he'd say if he could 'ear me calling him beautiful."

Lily raised her tear stained face, "We've got to get word to your dad."

"Perhaps the Navy could help," Maude suggested, "poor Dad, he'll take it so bad, I wish I could be with him." Tears began to roll down her cheeks again, "Poor little Lil, this'll break her dear little heart," she stroked his face, "Oh Jack, so many people loved you."

Apprehensively, Lillian approached the two women; it was only matron's insistence that gave her the resolve to face the family's pain.

She coughed softly to announce her presence, "Excuse me for intruding," both women looked up at her, "My name is Dove, Lillian Dove, I was with Jack when he died," her voice caught with emotion, "I was with him throughout the night."

Lily stood and took Lillian's hand in both of hers, "Thank you nurse. Did he speak with you?"

"He did, just before he died..." she sniffed back her tears, "...he said 'Give my mother my love, I know she's coming.'"

"Thank you for that," Lily covered her face.

Lillian went on, "But the thing is Mrs Cornwell, Jack had not been told that you were coming. The Commander sent for you but told us not to tell himin case...in case you couldn't come," she composed herself, "I think an angel must have told him."

*

The Post Corporal was always a welcome sight in any military establishment; contact with home was good for morale. Eli was the envy of many; he had three letters, and from the handwriting he was able to identify the individual writers. There was one from Lily, another in Arthur's spidery hand stamped by the Royal Engineers Postal Service and one from Jack.

After dinner Eli had his first opportunity to read his mail. He carefully sat on his bed, taking care not disturb his bed pack of folded blankets, and opened Lily's letter. It was the usual letter urging him to take care of himself and passing on local gossip and how much of a struggle life was on army pay. Arthurs was the small postcard that troops filled in prior to going into battle telling him that all was well; Eli said a silent prayer for his eldest son. He slit open Jacks letter with his penknife and read:

"Dear Dad, just a few lines in answer to your most welcome letter, which I received on Monday – first post for a week. That is why you have not had a letter for a long while. Thank you for the stamps you sent me. We are up in the North "somewhere" and they have just put me as the Sight-Setter on the forecastle gun".

"Cornwell!"the company clerk was standing by the hut door, he shouted down the billet, "Company Commander wants to see you."

"Now?"

"Now!" the clerk turned and left.

"What the hell can this be about?" Eli stuffed his letters into his breast pocket and followed the clerk.

"Could be promotion,Corny." Dick Acton called after him.

Eli knew that something was amiss when CSM Hulston knocked on CC's door and announced him without all of the screaming and stamping that was usually involved when seeing the Officer

165

Commanding; he was further alarmed by Captain Mills' behaviour.

"Have a seat, Cornwell," he indicated a chair in front of his desk. "You are no doubt aware that there was a major naval engagement in the North Sea the day before yesterday," he said when Eli was seated.

"Is it about my boy, Sir? Is it about Jack?" Eli felt an icy grip on his heart.

The captain's discomfort was written on his face, "Yes, I'm sorry to tell you that he was wounded during the battle..."

Relief flooded through Eli's being, "Wounded, oh, thank God it wasn't..." the words tailed away, he could see that his company commander had more to say.

"Let me finish, there's a good chap, this isn't very easy. Your son was taken to Grimsby Hospital the evening following the battle..." he opened a drawer and produced a bottle of Scotch and two glasses, poured two generous measures, handed one to Eli and took a mouthful of the other, "I am sorry to have to tell you that his wounds were extremely serious and he sadly died in the early hours yesterday morning."

Eli drained his glass and stood and saluted, turned about and walked from the office.

"Sergeant Major," Mills called.

CSM marched into the room with much crashing of hob nailed boots, "Sah!"

"Get a leave pass and travel warrant made out for Cornwell."

"Sah!" he saluted and made to leave.

"Hang on a moment Sergeant Major," the WO paused in the doorway.

"Cornwell's young son was killed in the big naval action the other day."

"Poor sod."

The barrack room was empty when Eli returned. He sat on his bed and took Jack's letter from his pocket and continued reading from where he had been interrupted by the arrival of the company clerk: '*Dad, I have just had to start in pencil as I have run out of ink, but still, I suppose you won't mind so long as you get a letter. I have got a lot more letters to send home and about so I can't afford much more and we are just about to close up the gun so this is all for now, I'll have more next time. I remain your ever-loving son Jack. PS: Cheer up Buller me lad, we're not all dead yet.*'

Eli's sobs could be heard by men passing the hut and those in adjoining billets.

*

As Ernest made his way tentatively up the longdrive towards the large house, through an open window, he could hear a piano playing *Bless this House*. It was a warm day and the peace of the large garden seemed somehow offensive and not suited to the news he bore. He mounted the steps to the huge oak door and pulled the bell chain.

Through the large bay window to his left he could see a girl seated at a piano. She had her back to him. Her long fair hair hung down her back and was tied at her neck with a black ribbon. The door was opened by an attractive girl in maid's uniform. She eyed Ernest for a moment and he half expected to be sent to the tradesman's entrance.

She smiled, "Good morning Sir, can I help you,"she asked in lilting Welsh.

"My name's Ernie Cornwell, I'm Jack's brother."

The smile was immediately replaced by a look that was a fusion of shock and dismay. She shook her head slowly, "Don't tell me..." her head shook faster and tears appeared in her large brown eyes, "...no, no." She suddenly took control of her emotions and stood back, "You'd better come in."

With his cap clutched in nervous hands Ernest followed Megan into the room where the girl was still playing the piano. The sun flooded in through the huge bay window warming his back and lighting the large and beautifully furnished room. The girl turned to face them as they entered. Ernest hesitated by the door his heart filled with sorrow and dread of the task in hand. He was surprised when the maid went across to the girl and took her in her arms for the girl was clearly not one of the staff.

Megan bit her lip trying not to cry. Her action alarmed Romin and her eyes darted from Ernest to Megan and back to Ernest. His serious expression and Megan's disturbed manner conveyed his dreadful message without a word passing between them. The inability of any of them to speak was overcome by Romin. She slowly stood up and broke free from Megan's comforting arms and walked slowly across and stopped inches away from him and stared up into his face.

"You are Jack's brother," it wasn't a question, more an accusation.

His hands were sweating and wiped them nervously on his cap, "Yes," he almost choked on the word.

Romin began to shake; Megan ran to her and put an arm round her shoulder. Romin closed her eyes and tears seeped under her long lashes. Suddenly she opened them and her grey green eyes now flashed angrily, "Well say something," she screamed, the tears flowed.

Ernest looked at his feet unable to face her anger, guilty that he was bearing such unbearable news and angry with himself for the feeling of guilt.

Megan rescued him. Romin's grief had given her some strength and control of her own emotion. She put her free hand on Ernest's arm and when she spoke it was gently and with understanding, "Tell us the worst, Ernie."

Ernest swallowed hard and tried to smile, "Jack was badly wounded on Monday," Romin looked up with a spark of hope in her eyes. Ernest swallowed again and screwed his cap into a tighter ball, "but he died last evening..."

Romin's shriek, as she fled the room, sent a dozen pigeons flying from the lawn into the large chestnut tree and brought other members of staff and Lady Carr – Langton, rushing from other parts of the house.

Chapter Fifteen

Monday the 6th of June 1916 was overcast and threatened rain for most of the morning. By the time the pitiful little cortege arrived at Manor Park Cemetery a fine drizzle had begun to fall depressing further the spirits of the mourners as they followed the cheap, pine planked, coffin the fifty or so yards to plot 323, where Jack was to be interred. Two score family members and friends huddled beneath umbrellas or braved the inclement conditions slowly soaking up the warm rain.

None of his shipmates had been able to attend and the only man in uniform was his father, in his thick serge khaki that, after ten minutes exposed to the rain, had lost all of its carefully pressed creases and resembled a sack of freshly dug potatoes. Eli had been shattered by his son's death, it was an event from which he would never recover, but as one serviceman honouring a brother in arms he bore himself proudly, in good military tradition, to Jack's graveside.

Pale and frail looking, Romin attended with Megan, both in black and veiled. On her left breast Romin wore the enamel sailor brooch that Jack had given her, the brooch she would wear for the next seventy years when she paid annual homage to the boy she had grown to love.

The service was simple and short, no hymns were sung, no bugler played the last post, no flags were in attendance to be lowered, and no Union Flag or White Ensign draped the coffin of the fallen youth. Jack was placed into the wet earth his sacrifice unrecognised and inadequately grieved over.

*

The day following the funeral, the day that Eli was returning to his unit, Lily received a letter from Captain Lawson that in some small measure alleviated their terrible grief and increased the immense pride they already had in their departed son.

It read; *Dear Mr and Mrs Cornwell, I know you would wish to hear of the splendid fortitude and courage shown by your son during the action on the thirty-first of May. His devotion to duty was an example to us all. The wounds which resulted in his death were received in the first few minutes of the action. He remained steady at his most exposed post at the gun waiting for orders, his gun would not bear on the enemy, all of the nine man gun crew were killed or wounded, and he was the only one who was in such an exposed position, but he felt he might be needed and indeed he might have been. So he stayed there, standing and waiting, under heavy fire with just his own brave heart and Gods help to support him.*

I cannot express to you my admiration of the son you have lost to this world. No other comfort would I attempt to give a mother of so brave a lad but to assure her of what he was and what he did and what example he gave.

I hope to place in the boys' mess a plate with his name on it and the date and the words 'Faithful Unto Death'. I hope that someday you may be able to come and see it there.

I have not failed to bring his name prominently before my Admiral.

Eli returned to his unit a very proud father.

*

Romin could not be consoled, she ate virtually nothing and could not be persuaded to take part in any event or show interest in any subject. Most of her day was spent in the garden with her sole companion, her dog Puck, and a Rudyard Kipling book. She told herself that her plight was not abnormal; so many families had lost more than one loved one but that knowledge did nothing to lessen the pain and emptiness that now engulfed her.

Unlike most big brothers, Clive had not only tolerated his little sister but he had enjoyed her company and they took interest in each other's hobbies and pastimes; though she always suspected that there was degree of pretence in his fascination with her childish pursuits. But as they grew they did develop genuine interests in the same subjects; the love of literature, of nature both flora and fauna and of history.

Her friendship with Jack had been a total mystery to her, she had liked him from the moment she had first seen him on that London street. Why he should have stood out from the masses she never could tell, was it the way their eyes met, the way he stared after her in awe? When she saw him in the back of the van at Sikkim she knew that they would be friends, fate had decreed it. Their stations in life, she accepted, were insurmountable but that did not seem to matter, they were natural friends whatever their accidents of birth. But once he had gone she realised her feelings for him were becoming much stronger and she would have sacrificed everything for him. Stubbornness and determination were two more qualities, or vices, that she had shared with Clive.

One week after Jacks funeral, hunger got the upper hand and she graced the breakfast table as normal but on this occasion she helped herself to a small amount of scrambled eggs and joined the rest of the family round the large mahogany table.

Sir James lowered his newspaper and peered over the top and smiled a smile of relief and welcome, "There is an item in the *Times* that will be on interest to you my dear,"

"Oh!" she looked up, interested, "Is it about..."

"Please Father," Violet protested, "if it's about..."

"The working class boy," Romin cut in anger in her face and voice.

"Would you like me to read it to you?" Sir James asked ignoring the developing battle.

172

"Please dear," his wife interjected in support of her elder daughter and her own prejudices, "not at the breakfast table."

Again Sir James ignored the protest and continued, 'It is an extract from Admiral Beatty's report to the Admiral of the Fleet, Lord Jellicoe. It reads thus: "'*A report from the Commanding Officer of HMS Chester gives a splendid instance of devotion to duty. Boy First Class John Travers Cornwell of Chester was mortally wounded early in the action. He nevertheless, remained standing alone at a most exposed post, quietly awaiting orders till the end of the action, with the gun's crew dead and wounded all around him. He was aged under sixteen and a half years. I regret to say that he since died*'."He paused and looked over the paper at Romin; she sat smiling her face awash with tears of pride and loss. He continued, "It goes on: '*I recommendhis case for special recognition in justice to his memory and as an acknowledgement of the high example set by him*'." Sir James folded the paper and placed it on the table and stood up, "Excuse me," he walked quickly from the room and as he passed Megan, who had entered minutes earlier with fresh toastand had witnessed the reading, he patted her on the shoulder to console her tears.

That same morning the *Daily Sketch*, though it did not appear on the Carr-Langton's breakfast table, carried the same report by Admiral Beatty under the bold headline;

BOY HERO BURIEDINCOMMON GRAVE – MISTAKE MUSTBE RECTIFIED.

After reporting the Admiral's words, it went on:'*Jack Cornwell's remains must not for ever rest in a common grave. The Admiralty will, we feel sure, see that the coffin is removed and a place found for it in a private grave with a tombstone or monument that shall give to posterity the story of how this brave boy faced death. An official of the Admiralty was placed in possession of the facts by the Daily Sketch last night and undertook to lay the circumstances before the authority. In the absence of any official action being taken the Daily Sketch would, of course with the parents' consent, be prepared to see that those remains are given a grave to which their honour entitles them.'*

Megan set the paper down, sought out a pair of scissors, cut out the article and placed it in an envelope. She then addressed it to Sergeant Joseph Clark, B Company, The Royal Fusiliers, REPS 43.

*

The hall was packed and the humid evening made the atmosphere a little uncomfortable. The average age of those in attendance was fourteen. The Boy Scout movement was eight years old and despite losing many of its scoutmasters to the military, it continued to expand and draw in boys from every walk of life. The current gathering was testimony to this fact, the Rally and Sports meeting that was taking place in Nottingham was being attended by more than three thousand boys and their leaders.

Lord Baden Powell, their founder was to make an important announcement this evening but the hall could only accommodate five hundred; only representatives of all the Troops at the Rally could attend. An air of excitement and anticipation filled the hall, a door opened by the stage and the buzz of voices ceased. In silence the great man, the Defender of Mafeking, mounted the steps onto the stage and was greeted by cheers and great applause. He was not a particularly big man but his presence filled the hall, he radiated warmth and strength. He raised his arms, smiling, and the welcome subsided.

BP stuck his thumbs in his belt and began, "I have two announcements to make this evening and both concern our fellow scout, Jack Cornwell," a ripple of applause, "As many of you will know, Jack has already received the Silver Cross for an act of bravery and this evening I am pleased and proud to tell you that young Jack is to be posthumously awarded the highest award at our disposal, the Bronze Cross." more prolonged applause. "As you know this award is rarely given and only for the very highest forms of bravery. This very evening it will be delivered to his parent's home."After yet more applause he continued."We all want to do honour to Jack Cornwell, the boy hero of the great fight in the North Sea, and to remind ourselves and our brother scouts after us, that he too was a boy scout. We might put up a statue or a brass plate but that would not keep his memory alive. So I propose to create a scouts badge for which a scout must be specially recommended and will be awarded for devotion to duty and physical courage." The applause this time was accompanied by a great cheer. When he had restored silence BP went on, "It will be formed by a simple letter 'C' of bronze,surrounding the scout badge. The 'C' will stand for courage and Cornwell and it will be known as the Cornwell Scout Badge."

Chapter Sixteen

Saturday the 29th of July 1916 was one of the hottest days of the year with temperatures reaching the high seventies. There was not the slightest breeze and the thousands who turned out on that sweltering afternoon wore their Sunday best in respect of the occasion. Suits, collars and ties were worn by the men and boys and women and girls wore dresses and hats of black. In the massed throngs many succumbed to the heat and the Boy Scout first-aiders were kept busy administering to those who were suffering from the heat and crush.

None of the Cornwell family had been over enthusiastic about the recent events, but public opinion was so strong that they had been overwhelmed by the strident calls for Jack to receive a funeral worthy of his sacrifice. The plea had come from all walks of life, from the children of his old school to the Mayor of East Ham, from leaders of the Church to a gaggle of politicians. The entire movement had been orchestrated and driven by the press, in particular the Daily Sketch and The Times.

Five days earlier Lily had finally given her consent for Jack's remains to be exhumed and a worthy funeral arranged. She had only agreed after recovering from the shock of a visit from Lady Jellicoe, the wife of the Admiral of the Fleet. She had barely been able to speak and Maude had been forced into the role of spokeswoman and hostess for the family. But it proved an easy and comfortable task,for Lady Jellicoe was a woman of immense compassion and understanding and was blessed with an unpretentious manner.

"That was just what I was hoping you would say," she said when Maude offered her a cup of tea, "that's extremely kind of you." When she had Lily's agreement to the exhumation and had sampled a second cup of tea, she took the cups to the sink and washed them.

Jack's heroism was on everyone's lips and in every paper in the land. His deeds were spoken of in every home and discussed in every public house. Every school in the country received, and displayed his photograph. He was held in the highest esteem throughout the services and he was regarded among his peers, both in the Navy and among civilians, as a glorious example of sacrifice and devotion to duty. His quiet heroism had impressed and endeared him to the nation, from his East End friends to those sitting in the House of Lords.

Although the country did not know it at the time, the biggest funeral of the First World War was about totake place. The cortege left East Ham Town Hall at three o'clock, led by the Band of the Royal Naval Volunteer Reserve and followedby a contingent of sailors, marching with arms reversed. The young hero's coffin, draped in the Union Jack, was conveyed on a gun carriage pulled by twenty-four ratings from his division and immediately behind it followed a dozen more ratings, including Jimmy and Bill, carrying wreaths. Then came two, empty, horse-drawn carriages, which were to pick up the Cornwell family at Alverstone Road. Behind the carriages for the grieving family followed a number more bearing, among others; the Mayor, Sir John Bethell Bart MP and Dr Macnamara, Parliamentary Secretary to the Navy. The cortege was further extended by representatives from a number of Scout troops and a detachment of the 10th Essex Volunteers. Bringing up the rear were lads from Jack's old school and other schools in the area.

The streets were eerily quiet; only the sound of slowly marching feet, horses' hooves, themetal-banded wheels of the carriages and the muffled drums, disturbed the warm afternoon hush. Occasionally, if the listener strained their senses, the sound of suppressed weeping could be heard. From time to time the band would play fitting hymns or martial music; Oft in the

Stilly Night, Solemn Melody and the Dead March, and it was playing the latter as the long procession passed through the gate of Manor Park Cemetery two hours after it had set off.

The grave had been prepared in the shade of a large chestnut tree and was surrounded by flowers. The Bishop of Barking waited by the graveside with a choir, made up from churches in the area, formed up behind him. Most of the public were held back at the cemetery gate but were able to witness events, and join in the hymns, as the burial place was only fifty yards inside the gate.

Six ratings lifted the coffin, still draped in the Union Flag, from the gun carriage, slow marched with it to the grave and placed it reverently on the planks that spanned the grave. The service began with the sailor's hymn; Eternal Father Strong to Save, and many a tear fell, shed by both men and women.

The Bishop moved to the head of the grave, "I am the resurrection and the life, saith the Lord, whosoeverbelieveth in Me, though he were dead, yet he will live; and whosoever liveth and believeth in Me shall never die."

The band struck up the hymn, Abide with Me and the congregation, including the masses outside the gate, solemnly joined in. Jimmy, still clutching his wreath grimly fought back the tears and Bill stood with his head bowed and shoulders shaking. A little to one side Amelia buried her head in her father's shoulder to stifle her sobs and just behind her Romin stood pale and severe with Megan's arm supporting her.

As the hymn finished Dr Macnamara stepped forward and spoke, "I have come to pay my tribute of respect to the memory of a hero, John Travers Cornwell, aged sixteen years, of His Majesty's Ship, *Chester*. He went forth with all his fellows in the sacred cause to which the allied nations stand committed."There was a ripple of disturbance as Lily,

178

who hadappeared to be in a trance since climbing into the carriage, slumped in a faint and was supported by Eli and Maude."The hopes and aspirations of early youth," the Naval Secretary continued, "the expectations of early manhood, the dreams of life, its affectations, its adventures and its opportunities. He laid all these down on the altar of duty." The sound of sobbing drifted from all parts of the gathering, all of it hushed. "He died inscribing his name, imperishably, upon the roll of British honour and glory. This grave shall be the birthplace of heroes. From it shall spring inspiration that shall make hearts more brave, spirits more dauntless and purpose more noble among British subjects yet unborn. John Travers Cornwell, will be enshrined in British hearts as long as faithful, unflinching devotion to duty shall be esteemed a virtue among us." He puffed his chest and raised his voice a decibel. "Think of him! Seek to emulate him! For by his sacrifice, and that of his goodly company of heroes to whom he belongs; heroes of land and sea and air. Heroes who sleep beneath the waves, on the plains of Flanders, amid the rugged slopes of Gallipoli and in the valley of the Somme, will the British ideal of freedom be maintained and flourish and not perish in our midst. The freedom they went forth and died for. By freedom shall their sacrifice be justified."

The bearers took up the weight of the coffin on the canvass straps, the planks were removed and Jack's remains were lowered slowly into the earth. The PO in charge of the firing party gave muted orders.

"Ready!"

As one, the firing party lift their rifle butts into their shoulders with muzzles pointing heavenward.

"Fire!"

The rifles crash out their salute over the silent crowd, three times and then the heart-rending sound of the Last Post reverberated in the soft summer evening air.

"Man that is born of woman," the Bishop began as the final notes faded away, "hath but a short time to live and is full of misery, he cometh up and is cut down like a flower." The mourners led by the family filed past the open grave. "Forasmuch as it hath pleased Almighty God," the Bishop continued, "of his great mercy to take onto himself the soul of our dear brother John, here departed; we therefore commit his body to the ground; earth to earth; ashes to ashes; dust to dust."

After the family had laid their wreath, Jimmy and Bill, both now composed, stepped forward and laid theirs, took a pace back and saluted proudly.

Postscript

At the start of the outcry for Jack to have a funeral worthy of a fallen hero, a fund was set up to provide the money to erect a monument to his memory, and to help his family.

A fitting memorial was erected at the head of his grave and was funded with contributions from scholars and ex-scholars from schools in East Ham. It is a cross supporting an anchor set upon a block on which the inscription is cut, the whole being eight feet in height. The dedication is:

IN MEMORIAM

FIRST CLASS BOY JOHN TRAVERS CORNWELL
VC
BORN 8TH OF JANUARY 1900
DIED OF WOUNDS RECEIVED AT THE BATTLE
OF JUTLAND 2ND OF JUNE 1916
THIS STONE WAS ERECTED BY SCHOLARS
AND
EX SCHOLARS OF SCHOOLS IN EAST HAM
It is not wealth or ancestry
but honourable conduct and
noble disposition that makes men great.

Sadly, the Cornwell family had not made their final sacrifice; on the 25th of October of the same year that Jack died, 1916, Eli passed away after a short illness, many who knew him claimed that he died of a broken heart. His name was added to the right face of Jacks monument. But still Lily's agony was not at an end, for Arthur, her stepson and Jack's half brother was killed in action in France on the 29th of August 1918. Like Eli, Arthur's details were added to the left face of the monument.

Jack was awarded the country's highest decoration for gallantry. On the 17th of November 1916, Lily went to Buckingham Palace and received Jack's Victoria Cross from the hand of King George V. Sadly, Eli died before the announcement was made about Jack's decoration.

The Navy League exploited Jacks heroism and raised a large amount of money to perpetuate his name,though when Lily approached them for help they turned her down on the grounds that the money had been raised for a specific purpose and the trustees could not divert money for other purposes.

Lily, therefore, only received a widow's pension of 10 shillings (50p) per week plus six shillings (32p) for Jack's pension. She received nothing for Eli's military service, even though he had served in the Egyptian and South African Wars. Lily had to support her daughter, Lil, and youngest son, George, on sixteen shillings (82p) per week.

She lost the house in which Jack had lived because she could not pay the rent and had to seek rooms in a refuge in Stepney. Lily became ill and was found dead, in her bed, on the 31st of October 1921, by her children.

Maude and her husband, who had been disabled in the war, decided to start a new life in Canada and sailed from Liverpool on the SS*Antonia* on the tenth of November 1923, taking Lil and George with them.

Read history and learn to love the soldier, hate the businessman and despise the politician.

Glossary

AB	Rank of Able Seaman
Andrew	Nickname for the Royal Navy
PO	Petty Officer
CPO	Chief Petty Officer
Dreadnought	The largest class of warship
HMS	His Majesty's Ship
LH	Rank ofLeading Hand
Log	Diary
NCO	Non-Commissioned Officer
Nozzer	Nickname for naval recruit
PT	Physical Training
PTI	Physical Training Instructor
Rating	All ranks below commissioned officer
Regulator	Naval police
REPS	Royal Engineers Postal Service
Rounds	Inspection
Salt	Nickname for a sailor
SBA	Sick Bay Attendant
Three striper	A naval rating with more than twelve years' service
White Ensign	Flag of the Royal Navy
Writer	Clerk

Printed in Great Britain
by Amazon

62204683R00111